PERSONAL
EFFECTS

Random House • *New York*

PERSONAL EFFECTS

A NOVEL

FRANCESCA DURANTI

Translated from the Italian
by Stephen Sartarelli

This work was originally published in Italian
as *Effetti Personali* by RCS Rizzoli Libri S.p.A., Milan, in 1988.
Copyright © 1988 by RCS Rizzoli Libri S.p.A., Milano.

Library of Congress Cataloging-in-Publication Data
Duranti, Francesca
[Effetti personali. English]
Personal effects: a novel/by Francesca Duranti; translated
from the Italian by Stephen Sartarelli.
p.   cm.
ISBN 0-679-41104-6
I. Title.
PQ4864.U68E3513   1993   853'.914—dc20   92-50514

Manufactured in the United States of America on acid-free paper
24689753
First U.S. Edition

Designed by Collin Leech

New York, Toronto, London, Sydney, Auckland

PERSONAL EFFECTS

*Quia igitur viro nec domina ancilla parabatur sed soci, nec de capite, nec de pedibus
sed de latere fuerat producenda.*

—Hugonis de S. Victore, *De Sacramentis*, Liber
I, Pars IV

Since man was given not a mistress or servant, but a companion, she had to be
drawn not from his head nor his feet, but from his side.

—Hugh of Saint-Victor, *The Sacraments*, Book I,
Part IV

•

AT FIRST I DIDN'T NOTICE the noise. It came from the landing and was like
the ever so soft gnawing of a mouse, mingled with the many creaks,
hums, and thuds of condominium life, and with the basso continuo of
the traffic five floors below.

A tiny little sound, the insinuating kind. It took a while to reach my
ears, working its way very slowly—and without my realizing, as I said,
since I'm not, after all, the suspicious type, unlike so many people I
know, who are thrilled whenever they can find confirmation of the
negative opinions they have of the outside world. Precisely because it
was so soft a sound, some time passed before it even registered in my

consciousness; and for the same reason, it set off an alarm inside me several minutes later. That sound was too soft—or to be more precise, it was too furtive.

I put my eye to the peephole and saw my illustrious ex-husband busying himself about the front door, in Missoni cardigan, corduroy pants, Timberland shoes, and ultraviolet-salon tan. I flung the door open; he practically fell into my arms. He was holding a tiny screwdriver in his hand. It looked to me like the one that had come with my Singer sewing machine.

"Riccardo! What the hell are you doing?"

I was hoping to make him feel like a thief caught in the act. Nothing doing.

"Oh hi," he said nonchalantly, almost surprised to see me materialize in the doorway to my own apartment. "I was just taking down the nameplate."

He had already almost finished removing the oval brass plaque with the name *Riccardo Prini* written on it in script. I merely stood there, breathless, watching him as he completed his work. There was nothing I could say to him. Riccardo Prini is not *my* name, after all; it's his. And once he attached it to his front door, in via Morigi, that sign would correspond to something real. In this elegant apartment lives Riccardo Prini, it would say. As for me—well, too bad.

"You could have rung the doorbell at least," I said. "The diskette is ready."

"I was just about to." In no hurry, he unscrewed the last screw and removed the nameplate. *"Voilà."*

We went inside. I turned on the computer, slipped the disk inside, and called up the file directory.

"There. Biographical info and quotations arranged according to subject. There's a ton of stuff here."

He wrote me a check that included alimony and payment for services rendered. The usual pittance.

"I need a plastic bag," he said.

In it he put the diskette and the brass plaque. "Take care now."

Bye-bye. End of scene. All in ten minutes.

I waited behind the door until the elevator took him away, then went out on the landing to have a look. In the spot where he had removed the brass plaque there was an oval of bright varnish newer than the rest of the door, the empty coat-of-arms of a person without a name. I gave in to my buckling knees and sat down for I don't know how long on the stair, to contemplate that melancholy heraldic crest. But I couldn't have stood back up anyway. I felt strange. Something had happened inside my head, a kind of explosion of horrible lucidity. Without warning, one of those little lights that illuminate dissecting tables had lit up. A cold, ruthless light—and I didn't like what I saw.

So that was how things stood. Things between Riccardo and me, that is, but not only. All things. The overall meaning of life, in short. I felt dizzy, sitting there like a fool with nothing left to my name: not even a name on the door.

Well, not nothing, really. I had the apartment, at least. It was my mother who had swayed me on that matter. "You can give in on everything else, but make sure you get the apartment."

And I know why. She was afraid I might move back into my childhood bedroom and interfere in her placid idyll with the good Federico. Actually, that wasn't the only thing she was thinking of, I suppose. She was also thinking of what's best for me, no doubt. Isn't that what mothers are always thinking of? Of what's best for their children? Of course, she's always very happy—and he too, I must say—to see me, to have me over for lunch, here in Milan, or even to put me up for a few days in their little, co-owned apartment at Lesa, on Lake Maggiore; but to have me around all the time—God forbid.

Well, they don't have to worry about that. There's no danger of that happening. But how tempting it was, at first. Going back home would have meant the whole thing had been a false start. We would begin all over again: soon the starter would fire another shot, and only then would this thing called life finally begin for Valentina Barbieri too. At age thirty? Of course, why not? And while waiting for the second shot, I could go back to the fold of my origins, to my mother's fragrance, her chaos, her cooking, our quarrels, our immediate agreement on some matters and our irreconcilable differences on so many others; lastly, I could even go back to a kind of new father, one more affectionate than the real one, living proof of just how lucky a woman my mother really is.

But I did not, thank God, give in to the temptation. And if, in the days following Riccardo's departure, the fact that our conjugal home had been left in my hands was only the smallest of consolations, it was a consolation that grew and grew, week by week. Every morning I could wake up and know where I was. That was already something. The bed was the same one in which I had slept for ten years beside Riccardo. The kitchen was the same one in which I had cooked $365 \times 2 \times 10$ meals for him. The corner by the window, with desk and computer, was the same one in which I had selected and input hundreds of theological texts—*De virginibus velandis, De mortibus persecutorum, De ira Dei, De sex alis cherubim, De planctu naturae*—for him to use in his brilliant biographies of the Fathers of the Church; the very same corner in which I, too, when I had the time, had worked a few half-hours on my article about Bohaboj Atanackovic, which I never finished. Later, in fact, thinking back on my choice of subject—an author dead at age thirty-two who hadn't had the time to write more than one novel—I realized it had been dictated by my anxiousness to be done with it quickly so I could get back to more serious things: his things.

As I went back inside, however, closed the door behind me, sat down at the kitchen table, and began distractedly to eat some leftover omelet, I thought to myself that it was really incorrect to call the life I had lived in that apartment *my own*. It was no more mine than the name just removed from the door. What difference did it make, therefore, that those two rooms plus kitchen and bath were registered under my name at the Milan land registry?

I looked around—around the house and inside my mind—and seemed unable to rest my eyes on anything I could really call my own. I have nothing of my own, I said to myself. Or not enough, in any case. There are not enough things around me to perform the task of protecting me, delimiting me, defining me, to serve as predicate to my subject, to give me a sense of being less—how shall I say—less amorphous. I went to the fridge to see what there was: I grabbed a tube of anchovy paste, some butter, two slices of pumpernickel, and a glass of wine, carried it all to the table and began to eat.

What was becoming more and more clear to me, as I stuffed my gullet like a Strasbourg goose, was that my bread, my butter, and my psychosomatic disturbances were not enough possessions to ballast my existence properly. I had to be able to call something else my own as well . . . I'm not sure what. I felt as if there were, on my person, an empty oval like the one on the door, a hole instead of a soul, with nothing inside. I had no occasion—nor had ever had any—to really say *mine*, or to think *mine*. My this, my that, my here, my there. For the first time, now, I could see that the inescapable upshot was no longer knowing where to begin to say *I*. That was it. Who ever said one must choose *between* Having and Being? Rather, one must Have in order to Be! I didn't *have* anything any more, thus *was* not anything anymore. Period. Even when I looked back in time, I could find nothing solid to set my eyes on and say, Look, that's me. All I could see was fog. Me? What's that? Who?

There was no more milk in the fridge. I went out, walked about a hundred yards to the supermarket, then—instead of going in—I kept walking a ways along the via Feltre and slipped into Lambro Park.

I circled round the little hill and then entered the densely wooded area where Riccardo used to bring me to make love when I was twenty years old. At the time all I knew about romance was what I had learned from the movies, and I can't honestly say that real passion stirred inside me. I wished for certain things, yes. For example, I would have liked, after our lovemaking, to turn onto my side and utter something very clever and witty. I would have liked my hair to fall to one side, covering my cheek like a curtain of silk. I would have liked for everything—my words, my hair, the glow of my fair skin, my boyfriend's gaze, the shaft of sunlight through the trees—to come together and bear witness to the same mysterious peak of emotion that Faye Dunaway always managed to express in similar circumstances. I hoped, in short, that sooner or later, I too might have my chance to enjoy the great Gift of Life, yet deep in my heart I heard no ticking that might lead me—like an infallible Geiger counter—to some sublime ecstasy reserved just for me.

Riccardo wanted something different, and he knew exactly what it was. He thought about it all day long and dreamed of it at night. He had just arrived in Milan after graduation from the DAMS school of the arts in Bologna, and in his head there was only room for the mirage of success. His restless desire to make it was written all over his face. He was thin in those days, always tense, avid, attentive, his ears pricked and his nose in the air, like a pointer, ready to seize all opportunities.

And the opportunity came one day, right in the park, under a nettle tree with branches almost down to the ground, in our little lovers' nook. He was smoking with his back against the trunk while I shook the ants off my clothes.

He was talking about money. It was his favorite subject.

"If you want to sell something," he said, "if you seriously want to sell it, to make good money, there are only two ways to go: to reach out to the public and give them the rubbish they like best, or else to create a false elite and feed it with false pearls. Nowadays the first way is the more prevalent one, but I can sense from certain signs that the cleverest people are beginning to discover the second. You have to take the public aside, put your hand on their shoulders and say, 'Let's go a little farther. Everyone else, they're all so common, so conventional, old-fashioned, provincial. You, you're different. I know that because I can see that you buy—or are about to buy—my products: my wine, my jackets, my magazine.' Then, of course, the wine, jackets, and magazines that you give them, it doesn't matter what they're really like. The public is in love with them, they're in no position to judge. All that matters is that those products bear the mark of, you know, the 'unusual,' the 'select few.' And it also doesn't matter whether the mark corresponds to the reality: it merely has to be a very visible sign, to keep that wink of tacit understanding in a state of perpetual tension, and to prevent that coaxing smile, which nourishes the love, from ever letting up, even for a second. 'Just you and I—you the buyer, I the seller—just the two of us, heart to heart. We the special, the ones above the crowd.' You have to play on their secret taste for unfairness, you see, their scorn for their fellow creatures, and then sell it like an expensive perfume. It takes intelligence, of course, and good taste. It's not some little game that just anyone can put together."

At that point he became animated. He was beginning to glimpse the sparkling of his vein of gold. He began to make plans and then discard them. For almost all of them a great deal of capital was necessary to get started, and he had only his stipend as substitute teacher of literature. This won't work, that won't work either. But his excitement grew: "It's all a question of formula, you see."

I did not see, and even now that he has found his formula and become rich, I still don't see what difference there is between him and a good old-fashioned hustler. But then I never studied at DAMS.

He hit upon it while smoking his third cigarette. At first a bit wary and hesitant, he quickly grew more and more convinced: "Let's say you're putting together a book," he said. "A good book, if possible, though that's not absolutely necessary. The important thing is that it be easy to write and not require any talent to speak of. No inspiration or nonsense of that sort. Two hundred pages or so, compiled by pillaging some forgotten corner of a library. And it should also be very easy to buy, needless to say, a coffee-table sort of book. But rather arduous to read. Am I making myself clear?"

"Clear as mud," I said. "How could it be easy to write and difficult to read?"

"Easily. In fact, I'd say there's a relation of direct proportion between the two. Anyone can see that. Being difficult is easy: being easy is what's difficult. Try explaining Dante's *Purgatorio* to thirty pimply blockheads: if you don't care whether they understand you or not, you can lecture with one hand tied behind your back. You can tell them whatever you like, and whoever gets it, fine, whoever doesn't, too bad. Don't you agree?"

"I don't know. But go on."

"Well, that's it. With a bit of luck, it might work. We just have to hope the slot machine turns up the winning combination."

He stood up and began to walk on top of the little mint plants that carpeted our love nest; with each of his steps the air filled with a scent of sautéed mushrooms, which until that moment I had always associated with images of romance and from that day forward became linked in my memory with thoughts of career, success, and money.

"It all depends on finding the right subject for that sort of endeavor," he said.

And, may God forgive me, I'm afraid it was I who, in the shade of that nettle tree, set off in his mind who knows what odd chain of associations that helped him find his inspiration.

"You would need a general theme," I said. I was no idealist, but the wily glint that shone in Riccardo's eye seemed wicked to me. I wanted to steer him away from the road he was so enthusiastically about to take, to trip him up by throwing a paradox at his feet. "Something that would make it possible to follow up your initial success with books of the same sort. Sort of like *Lassie Come Home.* At the priests' movie theater near my house when I was a little girl, they used to show a Lassie film every week."

It must have been the reference to priests, I guess. Whatever it was, Riccardo, on hearing my words, bolted up at me like a spring. "Patristics!" he shouted. I, at the time, didn't even know what the word meant. "How's your Latin?" he panted, all excited. "Well, you can brush up on it, if need be. Because we do need it. You can file all the information into a computer, I'll play around with it a little and make a biography out of it. Two, three, ten biographies—secular, irreverent biographies—of the Church Fathers. It's the most obvious thing in the world! Fantastic. After the first one, we can coast the rest of the way." He shook me, then hugged me. "We're all set, Valentina."

"But I can hardly remember my Latin, I don't know how to use a computer, and I'm sure they cost an arm and a leg," I said. "And don't forget I still have six finals to take."

In the end we did just what he wanted. We used all of his money, all of mine too, and a loan from my mother, to buy a computer, which in those days were very expensive. I learned how to use it, and I brushed up on my Latin. We got married, set up house as best we could, and several years later Hugh of Saint-Victor came out. I even found the time to graduate, but not to write my article on Bohaboj Atanackovic. And no children, of course, since from the start they had been postponed until we were able, as Riccardo put it, to coast. Then once we began to coast, he rolled over while coasting, and that was the end of that.

The nettle tree, ten years later, was still there, but rather than having grown, it seemed smaller. The mint was blossoming, between one lilac and the next. I didn't like the place; it brought back bad memories. Why had I gone back there anyway?

I began to make my way out of the park, toward the Metro station. Some fifty yards ahead of me was a girl walking her two dogs—a dachshund and a big bushy beast of indeterminate breed. The three were heading toward the pond; she was walking with a bouncy, self-satisfied step, a loping stride, visibly aggressive, that seemed to say: Look at me, I walk like a man.

But it wasn't just the gait that struck me. Maybe it was her blue shirt, tails hanging out of her pants and knotted together in front so that it billowed out like a wind-jacket. I don't know. Maybe the shirt, the sneakers, the dogs. Or maybe it was something that had nothing to do with her, but rather with that strange lucidity that was now making me see everything in enlarged form, slowed down and horribly meaningful. I thought of the little apartment she must have, near a Metro stop on line 2, the one that goes to the park; I thought of her bed, the yogurt in the fridge, her habits. You can't own two dogs in Milan without having an organized system of habits. I can't quite say what came over me, I only know that I felt a lump in my throat, and a great deal of envy for that girl. She had a life. She had a lot of things. She had the essentials, at least.

As I headed toward the park exit, I told myself it was impossible to know exactly how much stuff it was necessary to surround one's soul with to pass from the state of being someone alive, like me, to that of being someone with a life, like the girl with the two dogs. Nobody, I realized, can say just what the right measure is. One does not go from having too little to having too much by way of some binary in-out process of the sort that runs my computer. If that were so, I told myself, one could determine the point at which everything clicks and know the minimum amount of Having needed to ballast Being properly. One could then formulate, in rigorous fashion, a moral law against greed and all forms of undue lust. That much is permitted—they would tell you—and you can even have a little more if you like, as a margin of safety. But then that's enough, anything more is too much. Hands off: otherwise there will be nothing left for the others.

We would know the measure of right, like the right amount of salt in the soup, without having to go and trouble so unreliable a faculty as the conscience, and without having to resort to vague formulations like those of the Church Fathers when they say that yes, one may desire material wealth, but one must do so with a sort of elegant detachment, whereas only spiritual wealth should be pursued with tenacity. I suddenly realized how utterly powerless philosophy and ethics are in their attempt to keep man balanced on an impossible razor's edge. Once out of this shell-less, larval state of mine, one immediately rolls over to the other side. Look at Riccardo, for example. He wants everything. Everything is indispensable to him: success and money, along with the right not to have to work too hard; the bourgeois luxury car as well as that intellectual's aura of open-mindedness; brilliant friends and useful contacts; chic new girlfriend—an economist, no less—and me too, for whatever use he might still make of me: you never know. I think he wishes I could be kept under a plastic cover, like a disconnected computer, ready to be put back to use when necessary.

I could either go back home and stuff myself with frozen crêpes or stop by my mother's for a plate of pasta. I called her up. May I come by for dinner? Of course, she said.

I got on the Metro and sat down in a corner. I kept thinking about Riccardo and all the things he had so ravenously snatched away—and about myself, who had ended up with nothing. And as the subway train was plunging underground between the Cimiano and Udine stations, I came to the new and frightful realization that things could not have turned out any other way but the way they had, or the opposite way; and that at every crossroads in life, man is forever condemned to fall irretrievably down one side or another of a watershed between two opposite and equally dreadful abysses. The third alternative was only an optical illusion created by the unrealistic naïveté of my young age. I felt short of breath, as though opening my eyes for the very first time onto a world made up entirely of roller coaster tracks, where it was useless to try to maintain a position of reasonable equilibrium even for a second. And as though the subway train itself had transformed into a coaster-car, I abandoned all resistance, letting myself be dragged down into the bowels of the earth, my heart in my mouth and my head full of cotton, resigned and powerless, until I almost fainted.

Federico had not come home yet and my mother, in her Afro perm and flouncy, floral-print gypsy skirt, was playing solitaire under a faux Tiffany lamp.

I had never seen her dressed or coiffed any other way since the day she stopped crying, a couple of months after my father left her, and bought an unconventional necklace from a hippie sitting cross-legged on the sidewalk of the seaside promenade in Lerici.

I was just a little girl but I remember those times very well. In those days when a woman was jilted by her husband, her female friends responded with neither the companionship of yesteryear nor the indifference of today; the abandonment suffered was a badge of merit, an injury sustained in the field of battle, and a kind of celebration, a perpetual Bastille Day, usually broke out around the victim. My mother, for the mere fact of having been jilted by Papa, had been transformed in the eyes of her girlfriends from an ordinary woman—a cashier in a café—into a kind of queen. Her friends would come visit her at home—I remember it as if it were yesterday—and would sit on the floor, discussing things late into the night. They would drink white wine and eat potato chips, huge bags of them that my mother would buy wholesale from the dealer who supplied the café.

Without realizing it, my father, when he abandoned everything and went off to be a farmer on the farm of his forefathers in Umbria, had chosen a most favorable moment in which to disappear to the regret of none. My mother was left to herself in the golden age of feminism, when solidarity positively dripped from the tree trunks and wild slogans fell like fruit from the branches. She liked her new situation. Even later, after she went with Federico, and even after she married him, she always maintained that attitude of the unattached woman with no commitment to anyone. For this reason, while on my way to see her—she was my mother after all, I didn't have anyone else—I was well aware I shouldn't expect her to play too large a role in my drama. She had no trouble adapting to her own solitude, and it irritated her—as if there were a lack of good will on my part—to see me so incapable of adapting to mine.

It was no use telling her—though I had already told her a thousand times—that washing one's stockings at night in a deserted one-bedroom apartment with the TV broadcasting romances, marriages, and Texan love affairs is quite a bit different from taking to the streets with other women to burn your bras while shouting in chorus, "My uterus is mine, I can manage it fine." She herself doesn't realize how good she had it, in her day.

She had a world of fun, and in fact she has never since wanted to go back into the pitiful shell that had contained her until that moment.

She was a lot plumper before the separation, her hair always stiff with spray and cut in the shape of a little Dutch bonnet. It was important to her to be always neat. She had a very fancy hairdresser, but always got her hair done for a special price. The hairdresser was a friend, and her Salon de Beauté was right across the street from the café where my mother worked—that way mother could go there every Saturday from one to two in the afternoon. She still goes there, in fact: no longer to get her hair done, however, but rather to get it undone, now that she's changed her style.

Evenings, when she used to come home from work, she would stand for ten minutes in the shower then sit down in her bedroom at a vanity table covered with pink tulle, and as she rubbed glycerine jelly into her hands she would make me recite my math tables and history lessons. A little later my father would come home, briefcase in hand, from his job as representative of pharmaceutical companies; she would run to meet him, anxious and fragrant. He would make comments on the stories he saw on the evening news. He would say things like: "How can we go on like this?" or "What we need is the death penalty," and "I'll give them their flowered shirts and long hair!" Mama would agree with him and circle round the table with the serving bowl, filling his plate first, then Grandma's, then mine, then her own.

It's not that she was a different woman then, different from the one she is now: she was another woman altogether.

She has actually been three different women. And she has had three different lives: as good little wife, as feminist, and as remarried woman, on new terms. For when Papa left us she got an Afro perm and suddenly had a new life. Or a new soul, if you want to call it that. And she went out and got it from her hairdresser friend.

"Take back my devoted, wifely soul and give me one with self-awareness." She started wearing flouncy skirts with elastic waistbands, always cotton, with floral prints, both summer and winter. When it's cold outside she wears woolen panty hose and Russian-style boots. And of course she bought that necklace from the hippie—bought one for me too. It was an Easter Monday. I never wore it; so she ended up wearing that one too.

Federico, the companion of her third life, has since given her more such necklaces, and continues to do so—necklaces of wood, of straw, of tin, of silver, of seashells, of stones—so now she has a whole collection of them. She hangs them from her mirror, in that bedroom of hers that looks like a fortune-teller's den with its Indian bedspread, peacock feathers, potpourri of dried petals in a blue glass goblet, zodiac wheel framed in Murano glass, sticks of incense, shelves full of books on magic.

She put Jack, Queen, and King down on the last pile and set down the deck of cards. "Everything all right?" she said.

"Hardly. Today Riccardo came and took his nameplate off the door. He brought a little screwdriver and without saying a word to me, he started to unscrew it. Like a thief."

"What do you care? You're name's not Riccardo Prini, is it?"

"That's what I was thinking too. But it was a nasty thing to do anyway. He's just a lout. He could have easily had one remade for almost nothing, without having to stoop so low."

"But what do we know? Maybe he was very attached to it. You're always too quick to judge."

She, on the other hand, never judges anyone. Everyone has his own inscrutable reasons for doing what he does; good and evil don't exist, or at least they're not identifiable: everything has its purpose. And when someone's behavior is truly inexcusably mean or stupid, there's the final indemnity: "That's his business. *It's his choice.*" The most idiotic statement of all, the idiot's favorite. What isn't a choice? True, my heart doesn't beat by my choice, my nails don't grow by my choice, but everything else, every last act of mine, from the wisest to the most foolish, is always the result of a choice. Choice doesn't mean a thing: it doesn't excuse stupidity or wickedness. Oh it's a fine word, nice and slippery, but it doesn't mean anything. Everyone chooses and everyone, after choosing, invariably lurches beyond the choice made: whoever gives up will always give up more and more, whoever makes demands will always demand more and more, whoever has little will always have less and less, whoever has acted in a vile manner will always become more and more vile . . . Only by a great effort of will did I stop this train of thought, as if wrenching myself out of a whirlpool.

"He's a lout," I repeated, "and I can't stand him."

"Thank God you don't have to stand him. Fortunately you're separated."

"I can't stand being separated. No, that's not true, either. I just can't stand it anymore . . . But I don't know what 'it' is. I have to do something."

"That's what I've been preaching to you for the longest time. You can't stay cooped up at home all the time, waiting . . . For what? For the phone to ring, I guess. For Riccardo to tell you it was all a mistake, to pretty yourself up and get the pasta ready, 'cause I'm coming home. My dear, you're acting like a fool. Do you want me to read your tarot?"

"No, Mama. I think I need more than the tarot."

On the table—and obviously never opened—lay the book I had given my mother for her birthday. It was Milos Jarco's latest novel: *The Answer.* The title seemed almost a mediumistic message. I picked the book up. On the jacket flap was a photo of the author—beard, black-framed glasses, and a big smile full of gentle, ironic wisdom much more mature than his twenty-eight years.

And what if he actually did have the answer? I could go and look up Milos Jarco . . . The name, the face, the novel's title: all of it seemed more than promising—it seemed decisive. After all, this man managed to get on well with the East as well as the West, with the harshest of critics as well as the general public; might he not have found, between equally inaccessible peaks and gorges, a heavenly plateau to make his home? Did he not perhaps represent, in himself, that miraculous balance I had always believed in and which suddenly seemed to me a mystification, a children's fairy tale?

"Mama," I said, "I have to find a job."

"No kidding. That's what I've been telling you for the last ten years. A job of your own. It was sheer madness slaving away for Riccardo. What have you got to show for it?"

"Maybe I could write a feature for *Charme* magazine. The editor's a friend of yours, isn't she?"

"She was one of the group, yes, in the good old days. What sort of article would you do? There's no guarantee she would publish it, even if I do know her. It's not that easy, you know."

I was beginning to feel the way Riccardo must have felt ten years ago, when the inspiration for his career was just starting to come to him, under the nettle tree.

"I'm going to give it a try. If *Charme* won't take it, some other magazine will. I want to go interview Milos Jarco."

"Who?"

"This man here." I showed her the photo. "He's one of the great literary phenomena of the last ten years. A great, non-dissident novelist from behind the Iron Curtain. What do you think?"

She began to shuffle the cards mechanically, in silence. "I'm afraid he's probably been interviewed by thousands," she finally said.

My heart sank. She was right. And yet . . . "But I know his language," I said. I didn't give her time to make the most obvious objection. "I know everybody uses English these days, but suppose I don't do the usual sort of interview with him."

She gave me a look of doubt. "So you want to do literary criticism too?"

"Of course not. All that useless effort to squeeze something out of Atanackovic convinced me long ago that I wasn't cut out for that. I'm not a Slavist, I'm well aware of that. I'm just someone who had a grandmother from Istria and was therefore able, without much effort, to get a degree in Slavic literature and languages. That's not much, granted. But it's something. I can get around fairly well in those countries, in all of them. Better in some than in others, but I get by all right in all of them, from Poland to Montenegro."

"And so?"

"So, maybe I can come up with a formula for something new. I could talk not just with him, but with his relatives, his former schoolteacher, his first girlfriend—with all those people who don't know English and whom no other Western journalist has interviewed. Don't you see? I could write an article much different from the ones already published. If it's not for *Charme*, it will be for some other magazine. Someone will have to accept it."

After these minor events Federico came home, we ate *penne all'arrab-*

biata, and I went back home. Several days passed in which I hadn't even the time to think, what with all the travel preparations and red tape—visas, leave of absence from the Istituto Glossa where I teach Russian six hours a week, packing. But essentially, the preliminaries end here.

This is where my journey begins. And my story.

Ecce humana anima, tot honestata bonis, in principio suae conditionis.
—Beati Odonis Cameracensis Episcopi, *De
Peccato Originali*, Liber II

Behold the human soul, bestowed with so many good things, at the beginning
of its condition.
—Odo, Bishop of Cambrai, *On Original Sin*,
Book II

•

''THE ONLY ESSENTIAL THINGS, aside from clothes," you
said, "are instant cappuccino and a camp stove." Whereas I have also
brought along a camera and a tape recorder, which I've left sitting on
the passenger seat with the "rec" button always turned on so I can
record whatever comes into my head. And a plaid blanket, an inflatable
mattress, a traveling iron with retractable handle, a supply of American
instant soups, a sewing kit, a plastic food-container to be kept always
full of water, another container with a safety catch, for the gasoline
supply, ten meters of rope, and five hundred contraband dollars hidden
in the jack case in the trunk. In case of need.

It irritates you, I know, to see me leave with so much equipment in tow. You're sarcastic: "If your cargo shifts you'll drift like a Greek ferryboat," you say. You, at my age—when going off to your marches, meetings, and collectives—would bring only your toothbrush, your own indispensable feminity, and nothing else. A few times you brought me along too, when you couldn't leave me with Grandma, like the day when you all spread your legs to examine yourselves and one another to gain awareness of your own bodies and overthrow the phallocratic power of the gynecologist.

I myself am incapable of going away so bold and lighthearted. Like you, with your gypsy skirt. Like the girl with the dogs in Lambro Park. Your kind is sustained by . . . I don't know what. One can see, in any case, that your souls are sheathed just the right amount, even though for everyone, yourself included, I think, it would be difficult to say where the soul ends and the outer furnishings begin, with all due respect to Odo of Cambrai, Alan of the Islands, Pierre Abelard, and all the other Fathers of the Church.

You yourselves, venerable doctors, whom I have so often catalogued and committed to computer memory, try to take a soul of your choosing, with all its fine trimmings—body, clothes, name, cat, family, job, VCR—and put it under a ham slicer, taking away slice by very thin slice. Don't forget to stop every now and then and rotate it a few degrees, so as to strip its flesh uniformly away from that famous core. You should, eventually, reach the point where the blade itself will refuse to cut any more. You should see the blade dissolve, disintegrate, when— having removed all the unnecessary—it finally comes into contact with the divine nucleus, with the thing that says and is "I," with that marvelously hard substance, that truly unsplittable atom, as the ancients, your masters and ours, conceived of it.

I, however, am convinced that the "I" already begins to fall away with the first slice as, spread out on the waxpaper in unrecognizable strips on one side, it grows smaller and smaller on the other side, becoming slowly unrecognizable there too, to all and especially to itself, until it becomes impossible to tell just where this thing that says "I" might be—or if it ever even existed. And at that point the only thing left to do is to conclude the experiment by throwing it all into the garbage.

This is the first time this thought has spoken to me so clearly in my mind with such an awful ring of truth. But I once dreamed up something similar when I was a little girl. Catechism, at the time, was explained to me by my Istrian grandmother. I remember one evening we were sitting round the kitchen table shelling peas into a white and blue bowl, and she was trying to answer my questions.

"The soul," she said, "cannot be seen or touched, sweetheart. It's inside, hidden. It's the thing that makes each one of us what we are."

"So if I cut off one of my arms," I asked, "will my soul stay inside my body the same as it was, or will a little of it go away inside the arm? And what if I cut off more? And even more than that? When does the soul end up all outside of me?" Perhaps I had a premonition that one day destiny would lead me to live for ten years off the works of the Church Fathers. Or perhaps I already had a bent for tortuous arguments. Whatever the case, I was beginning to suspect that the soul, in order to survive, needed a bit of flesh around it. Whereas now, with that cursed new lucidity that came into my head when I sat down on the stairs to contemplate my nameless front door, I clearly see that not even flesh, by itself, is enough to keep it afloat.

You lent me your car. The other one, the one that used to be half mine, was taken by Riccardo like so many other things. Like all the other things, except the apartment.

The cargo is in order. "I've filled up the tank and changed the oil for you," you say. You hand me the keys, give me a kiss, and stand on the sidewalk following me with your eyes—an ever-diminishing figure in the rearview mirror, a gypsy telling fortunes on a street corner.

A long journey awaits me. Never before in my life have I driven a car for more than half an hour at a time. It was always you who drove me where I had to go, giving me the wheel only for stretches you considered a little safer; then I met Ricardo and married him, and after that it was always he who drove the car and everything else.

I have to cross three borders before reaching my destination. There are very few tractor-trailers on the road, and the late-summer traffic is moving in the opposite direction from me. I'm not a bad driver, for all that: I'm a bit slow, but safe. At any rate, I'm in no hurry. Perhaps one day—I truly hope—I'll have a real schedule, and my days off will be limited to a designated period between two specific dates. For now, however, I can take it easy. That's another reason for the extra five hundred dollars. When I get to my destination I want to look carefully around and not miss anything that might prove necessary to writing the sort of flawless article that the editor of *Charme* simply will not be able to turn down.

The Alps are getting closer and closer. Soon I'll have to cross them. I feel a sense of apprehension, almost malaise. Not surprising. After all, among all the people I know, there's not one who would venture into a foreign country without the comfort and protection of friends. I should add that my social circle is hardly the jet set—or if it ever was, it wasn't for very long: only from the time Riccardo became famous to when he began to ignore me and go out alone, crowning it all by jilting me for his sophisticated economist friend.

It's not really the first time I've ever left Italy; but to do it alone is a kind of adventure I've never before experienced nor even contemplated undertaking.

Perhaps it shows that I feel uneasy, and this makes me look guilty, like a smuggler. In fact, at customs they search my baggage with great zeal. In it they find three novels of Milos Jarco in translation, with his photo on the jacket flaps. They look at them suspiciously, then toss them unceremoniously back among my underwear.

But now it's done. I've crossed my first border, alone.

I have no trouble justifying the thrill of self-satisfaction running through me. Your inspiring muse, I am certain, crosses borders—alone or in company—without batting an eye. Well, I'll learn. Give me time.

I stop in a village to buy fruit and cookies at a store. Farther ahead, along the river, I turn the car off the main road and head toward its gravelly banks. I place the camp stove on a flat rock, turn on the heat, and make myself an asparagus soup.

The euphoria has passed. It's a beautiful place, but I prefer shutting myself up in the car to eat. Not that I'm afraid. The thought that someone could harm me doesn't even enter my mind. It's just that . . . I don't know. Here inside the car it's a little like being at home.

I drive another fifty miles along a deserted road. The first human settlement I come across is a large farming town. There's no possibility of stopping there for the night. "Further on," I am told. "About an hour down the road." I continue on my way through fields of corn and sunflowers until I reach a town with a small hotel. I am tired of driving. I carry all my things up to my room and barricade myself inside. It's only six-forty, and it's still light outside. I make myself a double cappuccino and dip half a box of cookies in it.

I also have a supply of suspense novels with me. I unwrap one of them, pulling off its plastic cover, and crawl into bed convinced I have been an utter fool to embark on this adventure.

All I can see, as I continue on my voyage, is that the rivers are wide, deep, and clean, and the roads atrocious. I stock up on water at a public fountain in one of the towns. I buy a hot salami and a loaf of dark bread; I'm also tempted by a wedge of soft ewe's cheese, but I decide against it, for fear of getting ptomaine poisoning. I immediately regret it, and so I stop in the next town and buy some cheese which, however, compared to the other one, seems less inviting, too seasoned and smelly. Nobody sells fruit, and I begin to feel like I'm suffering from vitamin deficiency; and yet everywhere around me I see trees filled with plums and apricots.

My left forearm, which is taking in every last bit of sun shining through the car window, is already tanned. I stop the car in an entirely deserted area, next to a pond inhabited by countless wading birds. I lie down near the bank, in a sheltered spot, roll up my slacks and close my eyes to get a bit of color. I eat some bread and salami, drink a cappuccino, then brush my teeth with the water in my plastic jug before heading off toward the second border.

I have crossed an entire country, six hundred kilometers, without exchanging a single word with a living soul except to obtain food and lodging. Nobody knows me here. I don't exist.

But tell me the truth, Riccardo, did I really exist at home? For you, I mean. I certainly don't now, but in my opinion I never did, not even at the start of our marriage.

I fold up the plaid blanket and put the methane stove, the red enamel pot, and the unmatched cup—the survivor of a matching pair, a wedding gift from I forget whom—back in the basket. It makes me feel a bit melancholy, because on it is written "His." But I brought it with me anyway, because it's very big and therefore very good for instant soups; and because it's made of an almost unbreakable porcelain—almost, but not entirely, since its twin, "Hers," broke many years ago.

"You don't need to go all the way up there," you said. "And you don't need to look for another job, either. In any case, you won't find one." Oh, is that so? So you really do think that, aside from my six hours a week of Russian classes at the Istituto Glossa, I can get along splendidly merely by slaving away on your biographies. "What else do you need, anyway?" you say. "You have a home, you don't have any children, and you eat like a bird."

To begin with, since you left I've been eating like a horse. And anyway, what if I suddenly got the urge to take a little trip to the Maldives myself, like you and your illustrious lady friend? What if I felt like buying myself a white fox-fur coat like the one you gave her? And get this into your head: once I'm finished with Lactantius I have no more intention of working for you. Find someone else. Your esteemed paramour can't help you, naturally, because she has to devote herself to "her own" things. You'll just have to shift for yourself. Aside from the wretched pittance you pay me, I don't like the idea of going to turn in the work and having to ring the doorbell under the nameplate that until six months ago used to be on my door, the nameplate that bears the last name that until six months ago was mine.

I've crossed the second border. Now there's a strip of land—with cities, rivers, factories, policemen—between me and my life. Between me and my mother, between me and Ricardo, between me and my house, between me and my television set.

I'm traveling along a kind of expressway, a bit more broken up than our own, but free. I continue to cover ground without exchanging any words with anyone, except to buy food and fuel. It's a stupid way to travel, and not worth talking about.

I'm not crossing this country: I'm hurdling it. What I see around me doesn't interest me. I wish I were one of those people who know how to enjoy the beauty of their surroundings, who every day have a new, unforgettable experience. Instead I always seem to be moving away from something without ever managing to come near to anything. I take off as if from the barrel of a rifle, fired toward my destination.

The sun is still high in the sky, there's no point in stopping to sleep: I continue on toward the final border. Another country has passed under this Volkswagen's tires, and nothing of it has stuck to me, not even its dust.

The policeman who checks my papers is wearing high black boots. He gestures for me to step out of the car and to follow him into his sentry post. He wants to know what I intend to do in his country. I show him my camera and tape recorder. "I'm going to write a feature article on Milos Jarco," I reply.

His suspicious face doesn't brighten in the least. On the contrary. He mutters something and goes into the next room, leaving me alone for fifteen minutes. When he returns, he slams his stamp down brutally on my passport, as if to kill a large insect.

To reach the capital I would have to continue northward for another half hour; my destination, however, lies two hundred miles to the east. I could easily make it before nightfall, but I prefer stopping in a little town dominated by a great smokestack with a plume of white smoke. I take a room in a hotel surrounded by a small garden. I bring only my toilet articles up to the room, leaving the food and hot plate in the car. I take a shower and wait for evening in my room, lying on the bed with the curtains drawn and the light off.

I've decided to eat at the hotel restaurant, but the place is so dreary that at the last minute I almost change my mind, which I would do if I weren't so famished. A couple is sitting at the table next to mine. "He wasn't sincere," she says. The man shrugs his shoulders without looking up from his goulash. "Everything would have turned out differently, if he had been sincere."

After dinner I go to the bar to drink a brandy. I buy a pack of cigarettes from the bartender; he lights one for me.

"Are you in business?" he asks.

"Yes," I answer. I don't know why I felt like lying.

"What line?" he asks.

"Camp stoves." The bartender pours himself a brandy as well. "It's my first time in this country," I say, "but I almost feel I know it already, from the novels of Milos Jarco."

I thought I could begin to gather some opinions on the great writer, but it doesn't work.

"I get off work at nine" is the bartender's reply. He smiles insinuatingly at me. He's bald, and wears a pin on his collar. He's not interested in literature, but wouldn't mind picking me up anyway. Too bad. I'll find out everything I want to know later on, when I reach my destination.

"I have to go," I tell him.

I wouldn't want that bartender to touch me even if I were dead, mind you; nevertheless, I feel a faint tingle running down my spine as I implicitly turn down his implicit proposition. I feel in a position of strength. A business representative, in the field of camp stoves, in an out-of-the-way hotel, with before her the choice of whether or not to allow herself a little affair. Let me put it more directly, without beating around the bush: I feel in a masculine position. That's the point. After all, how many hundreds of thousands of years is it that you've been giving us every reason to envy you this position of yours? It would be rather strange if we didn't.

I pass before the mirror in the dining room. I imperceptibly slow down my pace. Hm. Not bad. It's clear, my good man, that I'm not yet ready for the dustbin. You took my car, my work, and my last name, but there must be something left all the same.

I forgot to bring the suspense novel up to my room. I have trouble falling asleep.

3

Hoc vitium haeresim parit; schismata facit, generat suspiciones, inauditos concinnat rumores, colorat probra, palliat denudanda, denudat velanda.
—Alani de Insulis, *Summa de Arte Praedicatoria,*
Caput XXVII, "Contra Mendacium"

This vice breeds heresy; it creates schisms, arouses suspicions, gives credence to incredible rumors, color to calumny, hides what should be uncovered, uncovers what should be veiled.
—Alan of the Islands, *Treatise on the Art of Preaching,* Chapter XXVII, "Against Lying"

•

IT'S NOT SO MUCH A STREET as a public park, long and narrow, which flows like a tributary from the thermal baths at the foot of the hill, descends at a slight incline straight down through the whole city and empties into the river a short way from the tannery. The Hapsburg palaces lining it on both sides were built according to a single criterion, as were the fountains and buildings that follow one another at regular intervals in the middle of the tree-lined strip—music pavilion, aviary, natural history museum. The rest is a medley of little three-story rococo houses—in incredibly bad condition—mixed together with peeling tenements and tumbledown flats. Only the Hapsburg boulevard, the Promenade, gives a sense of order to the city, dividing it into two equally disjointed parts. The other streets have no rhyme or reason at all: they run for a while in one direction, then change their minds. The river—I could see its yellow curve upon arrival—barely touches the historic center of the city.

It's a provincial town, formerly on the outermost edge of the empire. From the little neo-Corinthian temple of the baths, with its scented honeysuckle vines wrapped around the columns, one can almost touch the opposite end of the town, down at the bottom of the Promenade, where the tannery lies crouched like an animal, fuming with poison.

The first thing I buy is a map, then get a room in a hotel situated in a tangle of little streets on the right-hand side of the boulevard, something that seems within my financial range but also sufficiently clean. I park in a dusty, desolate square, and unload all my things from the car. I ask the porter if he knows the address of Milos Jarco.

"Milos Jarco . . . I believe I saw him just this morning, in sweatsuit and tennis shoes. He's a very athletic young man, likes to stay in shape. You should turn right and go to the end of the street, cross the Promenade—" With his finger he points to the place on the city map that we've just spread out on his bench. "Then, from there, you should probably ask someone else. His house is on the other side of the boulevard, in this area here, more or less." He traces a rough circle on the map with his fingertip. "Or you could go to the headquarters of the Writers' Union, which is along the way, and ask them."

This seems like a good idea to me. The porter offers to accompany me there.

"I was just on my way out, and I'm going in that direction," he says. He rings a bell and leaves his post to a young man who appears from under a staircase with a book in his hand—an American novel in its original language. He removes his green smock and tosses it behind the bench. "Let's go, I'll walk you part of the way."

We dive into the labyrinth and through it, following apparently senseless routes for about fifteen minutes. We then resurface on the boulevard and cross it near the natural history museum. We immerse ourselves anew in the maze on the left-hand side and walk for another ten minutes. Suddenly the porter says, "This is where I leave you. Now you have to keep going another hundred yards or so until you reach that old building there, with the flag on the balcony."

The Writers' Union is on the third floor. There is an old elevator in a wrought-iron cage, but the sign hung from the doorknob informs me that it's not working. The sign seems almost as old as the elevator.

I climb the stairs and ring the bell of what must have once been the apartment of a fairly high functionary in the imperial bureaucracy.

A middle-aged woman walking silently in felt slippers takes me into a poorly lighted corridor.

"I'm an Italian journalist," I tell her. It's not true, naturally. There are, of course, a number of things that have appeared in Italian newspapers that were mine for the most part, but they bore your signature, and that's all that counts. On the other hand, I can't very well show up in a place like this saying—even if it's true—that I'm nobody, can I? How can I hope they'll pay any attention to me if I don't falsify my credentials? You capitalized on ten years of my labor in your name, and then took your name away from me—along with your clothes, the car, the silverware—by unscrewing the brass plaque on the front door. You sneaked up, like a thief, with the screwdriver to my Singer, and as of that moment I ceased to exist. I know—you don't have to keep telling me—I know I keep ruminating on this same theme. "If you care so much about it, put up another one," you said. "You can do it for a few thousand lire."

Not so fast, my friend. I prefer to maintain my every right to bear a grudge, if you don't mind. It's more complete that way. More satisfying.

"I've come to do a feature article on Milos Jarco," I continue.

"At the moment he's out of the country," she says. "They're making a film out of his last novel. In Hollywood. He's collaborating on the screenplay."

She's polite with me and shows me a magazine that she picks up from a table in passing. It has a photo of Milos Jarco with a famous American actress.

"See," she says, "he's away."

I try to hide my disappointment. It was the epitome of stupidity to come all this way without making sure, before leaving, that the writer was at home. You, Riccardo, would say I lack professionalism, your supreme, sacrosanct myth.

Meanwhile we have walked the entire length of the corridor and entered a large room with stucco decorations on the ceiling. It's furnished like a café, with groups of chairs around little plasticized metal tables. A dozen people or so, men and women, are sitting here and there about the room. A few of them are talking quietly, others are writing or reading.

"It doesn't matter if he's not here," I say. I decide to lie because I'm too embarrassed to admit to my idiocy. "Actually, I knew he wasn't. The article I want to write is on the places and people he knew in his childhood. His home, his grammar school, his mother. Perhaps his first girlfriend, his friends from the university . . ." Deep inside I'm hoping she's mistaken, that the photo in the magazine is an old one. After all, the porter at the hotel told me he saw Milos Jarco this morning . . . Of course: the secretary of the Writers' Union must be mistaken, I'm almost sure of it.

A very thin man dressed in brown approaches us. He has an odd smell about him that seems familiar to me, though I can't quite put my finger on it.

"Allow me to introduce our president, Professor Voytek Miczan," the woman says demurely.

I repeat my request. "I would like some suggestions," I say in conclusion. "On the jacket flaps there never is any mention of Milos Jarco's life before he became successful."

The other people in the room have gotten up and approached us. The president of the Writers' Union does the introducing. They are poets, novelists, essayists. They ask me about Italy: I have the impression they know more about it than I do—which wouldn't take much—but also more than you, and even more than your venerated queen of hearts, the intellectual in white fox-fur. They stand around me with a kind of feverish voracity; they mention Italian titles and authors, as well as literary magazines that—as far as I can tell—are known only to those who publish them. I manage as best I can, keeping to generalities.

They all talk at once, wanting to make a good impression on me and to look good in one another's eyes. Milos Jarco must be too familiar a subject, not suitable for displays of vanity. If I want to steer them in that direction, I will have to speak with them one at a time and lead them out of the exhibitionistic excitement my presence among them has aroused.

Right now it's useless to ask any questions. Moreover, I feel as though all the miles traveled have suddenly come crashing down on my back. I regret having come here directly, without lying down for an hour or so to rest. I wish I could run away and lock myself in my ugly hotel room.

But the president of the Writers' Union wouldn't hear of letting me go just then. He detains me almost frantically, his hand resting on my arm; he pushes me toward the center of the room while all the others surround me with a wall of smiles.

"Allow us to celebrate your most welcome arrival," says Professor Miczan. Pastries suddenly appear—big spongy balls swollen with geranium-colored liqueur—accompanied by cans of orangeade and beer. And lastly, a bottle of very strong anisette. The president proposes a toast to their gracious Italian guest, with the hope that she has appreciated their little impromptu celebration, and with best wishes for a pleasant stay.

Only the poet Ante Radek keeps a bit of distance. He was introduced to me with the others, but was the only one who didn't come forward to wish me well. I thought he had actually left, because I looked around for him and for a while couldn't find him. Now he has reappeared and is standing in a corner without speaking, but will not take his eyes off me. It almost seems that he likes me . . . Is it possible? Could a man so handsome possibly be attracted to me?

You, I can tell you myself, are not handsome. And let me also disabuse you of another illusion: it's not true that good looks don't matter in a man. They matter, and how. One can resign oneself to ugliness; but one still sees it, the very same way you see it. The same goes for the signs of aging. Even when you tore the name off my front door and I felt I would have accepted any sort of humiliation if only you had put the nameplate back and stayed with me, don't think I didn't see you exactly as you are.

I would have done anything to keep you from leaving, but my eyesight was perfectly clear. As was—since we're on the subject—my perception of my own feelings. So don't get too puffed up: what would have made me get down on my knees and grab onto the hems of your Missoni—if I had thought it was of any use—was not love. Panic, perhaps. Or I don't know what. But not love. Don't delude yourself.

Ante Radek is probably about my age, perhaps a few years younger, and tall and slender as a whip. He has blue eyes and airy blond hair that falls in soft curls. He is, of course, very poorly dressed: any worse would be impossible. Little brown suit, threadbare, with sleeves too short and shiny at the elbows; polo shirt with yellow and burgundy pinstripes; big mouse-colored sandals perforated with holes; short grey socks with red elastic bands. Perhaps if someone dresses so badly it's a sign that he himself is not aware he's handsome.

Or perhaps he's perfectly aware of it, and for this very reason is above the sort of petty vanity that for you, on the other hand, is your main prop—not so much for supporting the world as for grabbing the biggest slice of it possible. Or else the supreme laws, the great principles of gravity that govern this place are so different from those in force for us, that even the smallest things, like the sandals of the poet Ante Radek, should be interpreted according to standards entirely unknown to me.

If this is an upside-down world, then it is quite possible he likes me. And anyway, I don't see why I should discount that possibility, even judging by our own criteria. After all, he may not even notice the slightly long face, the melancholy expression, the few extra pounds of fat I've put on because of you, in my unhappiness—the kind of fat that comes when one sits curled up in an armchair and, without realizing it, puts away a box of crackers and a jar of mayonnaise during an episode of *Dallas*. He may only notice how stylish and cosmopolitan I am, compared to him. He may be drunk with the wind of the West I've brought into this dusty headquarters of the Writers' Union.

Do you see how much trouble I have believing I can be attractive to someone? How great an effort I have to make to muster up a little confidence in my charms? A fine mess you've made. Because it *is* your fault, needless to say. It's you who taught me that humiliating feeling of being something to be thrown out, like a piece of fruit gone bad. Do you remember? As you were packing your new designer articles into your suitcase, I begged you to tell me *why*—I was almost suggesting you make something up. And you only replied: "For no reason." Do you remember? "I just feel like leaving," you said. "I don't want to live with you anymore."

For heaven's sake: it's the best reason in the world. Let's also say it's the only real reason why people separate. It's just that hearing it thrown so brutally in one's face has a strange effect. Like thinking one is garbage. Like smelling bad. The whole way you treated me over the final years, and then that last scene, with me in tears and you all worried that your jackets might get wrinkled in the suitcase, made me feel ashamed, made me want to hide.

You, Mama, say, "Stop thinking about it. Don't torment yourself over it." Sounds easy. You came out with something you must have learned from some cultured friend of yours in the good old days. "At this rate," you said, "you'll lose your independent sense of identity. Your life is suspended waiting for external occurrences—telephone calls, miracles." I know, I know. Meanwhile, time keeps passing. It's awful. Going on from day to day without ever managing to bring to bed, at night, a reasonable number of hours, of the twenty-four through which I've just floated mindlessly, that I might call life. Not joy, not heroism or success. Just life. That's not asking so much, is it?

It's true that it was that way even before, when Riccardo used to take all my hours away from me, not to mention my days and years. Except that in those days I had the patience to wait. Because I was younger, I guess. Today no, I would tell myself, maybe tomorrow. What "no" and what "maybe" referred to I couldn't have said, exactly. "No," it wasn't worth the bother. "No," my useless time can't possibly be that much-heralded thing that people call "life." "Maybe" tomorrow something will change. Maybe tomorrow it will begin.

Now I feel I can no longer keep postponing, accumulating days of nothingness waiting for something to begin tomorrow. There are fewer and fewer tomorrows, and I can feel the day approaching when I will almost be able to count them, like a convict in his cell on death row: ten, nine, eight . . .

I now suffer from insomnia, have come down with dermatosis, I eat too much, smoke too much, suffer from phobias and anxiety attacks. I'm afraid, Mama. I'm afraid I'm going to find myself face to face with death when there's no time left for anything, knowing I've squandered those few moments so sparingly granted me—barely a flash between one darkness and the next. And not because I've frittered away the days in happy-go-lucky frivolities. But merely because I handed them over to Riccardo Prini, so that he could cull from them his brilliant biographies of the Fathers of the Church, and with them money, success, and his economist paramour. I can already feel the desperate wave of regret for my wasted life about to pounce on me, not so much like a wild beast lurking in shadow as like a tired mirror-image of myself hatching out of my self, getting up from the bed, and bending over my dying body to sigh in my face, with my very last breath: "Silly fool."

At any rate, the handsome blond poet is looking at me from his corner and I'm returning his gaze. Nobody feels like talking about Milos Jarco's childhood, and so we go on to discuss what is happening in the wide world around us, of which this town seems the most distant of outposts. By turns they stand up, clear their throats, and in my honor make a series of toasts, all very formal, solemn, and nearly identical. In the intervals between toasts they bombard me with questions. It's as though I were a merchant—a gypsy, or Marco Polo—passing through a village starved for news. They know everything about everything, and still they're not sated. They ask for news of Italian poets unfamiliar to me, and they even ask, old friend, about your biographies of the Fathers of the Church. I refrain from telling them how you originally got the idea that in a short time transformed you from a melancholy substitute teacher into a best-selling author, how the money and success began to pour in, how you started appearing on television and conducting morning broadcasts on the radio. Or how the last step in your climb was to abandon the one-bedroom apartment in piazza Udine and me and to replace us, respectively, with the penthouse in via Morigi and the beautiful intellectual.

The union writers know all your biographies quite well, although their familiarity with them does not go so far as knowing how much work of mine went into them. But I am content to shine with reflected light. "Riccardo Prini is my husband," I tell them, "or at least he used to be."

Aside from this, I have little to tell them. I am not a very good ambassador for Italian culture; I'm a little better when two women novelists question me on the history of Italian feminism. I grew up in the middle of it and know enough to give reasonable answers, although it immediately becomes clear that even about this subject they know much more than I do.

Only after two pointless hours does the party come to an end. There are still a few pastries on the trays, which the secretary wraps back up. We all go downstairs together and say our good-byes in front of the building. I still haven't understood whether Milos Jarco is in town or abroad, and I haven't been told a single thing of use to my project—no names, addresses, or information. Nothing. And yet everyone is very friendly and quick to declare his readiness to help me in every way during my stay in their city. Each of them gives me a calling card, which for some consists of a color photo—in black suit, tie, solemn expression, corpselike—with name, university degrees, profession, and address printed in very ornate typeface.

The poets, essayists, and novelists scatter each in a different direction, including Ante Radek, who walks away after having stared intensely at me, as if to communicate a message. Or so it seemed to me. The liqueur in the pastries has gone to my head, and on top of that I'm exhausted from the journey.

Only the president is left standing next to me. He still has that smell about him and is surrounded by a cooler layer of air, as if his clothes were damp. Now I realize what it is that he reminds me of: his smell is the same as the one that fills the shop when Paolo, my neighborhood butcher, opens the door to the cold-storage room and that cold smell of dead meat wafts out.

"I live rather near your hotel," he says. "I'll walk with you a bit."

He takes me into his icy atmosphere as into a vehicle and steers me through the tangle of streets. He speaks to me endlessly about contemporary Italian literature, leaving me no opportunity to ask him anything about Milos Jarco. The street we walk down looks different to me from the one I took with the hotel porter, but it takes us more or less the same amount of time. Not even the president accompanies me all the way to my destination. "This is where I leave you," he says at a certain point. "You must take the first left and then turn right."

He vanishes, taking his funereal aura with him. With great pleasure I breathe in the mild air, the vague odor of cabbage, dust, and soap pervading the neighborhood.

At the hotel I find the same young man with the American novel. "I'm very sorry," he says, "but you were given a room that in fact was not available. We took the liberty of moving your belongings."

"You moved my belongings?"

"Yes."

"What does that mean, you moved my belongings?" I feel dizzy. The morguelike stink of Voytek Miczan has dealt my tired resistance the final blow. I hold out my hand. "Let's have the key, anyway."

"We've moved you to another hotel, miss. Here there were no vacant rooms left, unfortunately."

"But I don't want to stay in another hotel. I feel ill and would like to go up to my room immediately."

"Everything's all right, please don't worry. You'll be fine in your new room. The other hotel is of a higher class than this one—much higher— and you won't have to pay any difference in price. I'll accompany you there myself. It won't take but a few minutes."

I find myself back in the street again, almost running as I strain to keep up with the assistant porter's long strides. We reach the deserted boulevard, walk along it a short bit and then stop in front of a monumental building with a roof all made up of domes and spires. At the front it has a great veranda enclosed by multicolored stained glass and two enormous, semicircular staircases.

"Here we are," says the assistant porter.

"Here?"

"Yes. Hotel Esplanade. It's the foreign hunters' favorite place, when they come for the stag hunts."

"But it's out of the question. It's undoubtedly too expensive."

"As I said, there won't be any difference in price from what you were paying at our hotel. It was our mistake. You mustn't worry about that."

"But surely the extras will be expensive . . . I don't think this is a good idea."

"Everything will be taken care of. Please don't worry."

He pushes me up the stairs, then turns me over to a porter in peacock green livery with gold galloons; then he disappears.

How dare they stick their noses into my things. I am very irritated that the staff of the seedy old hotel would entrust my camp stove and supply of instant cappuccino to these solemn attendants of the Hotel Esplanade. And the suspense novels. And my mother's old jalopy . . . Or perhaps they forgot about that.

"What about my car?" I ask.

"It's already safely parked in our garage."

This is a place for rich Western tourists, or very high party functionaries. It is the apotheosis, or a parody, of the capitalist style. A museum. A theater. The kind of place a lady traveling on the Orient-Express would come to stay, with her pigskin valises and a few glossy magazines in tow—*Vogue, Harper's Bazaar.* Maybe even a French novel. But certainly not with a plastic bag full of suspense novels. And, good heavens, not with another plastic bag with a wedge of ewe's cheese in it.

They've given me a huge suite. Anteroom with big, mirrored armoires, an antique, sumptuous bathroom full of tubes and knobs like a submarine, a tub with lions' feet. The bedroom starts with an enormous mahogany double bed surrounded by velvet curtains and then sprawls several dozen feet as far as the windows; between the bed and the windows there are sofas, armchairs, a *chaise longue,* and a presidential writing desk with a bronze lamp adorned with spread-winged eagles, tigers, lions, and other wild beasts. On a complimentary red leather folder bearing the words "Hotel Esplanade" they have put the camp stove, the cheese, and the rest of my provisions.

My instinctive reaction would be to try and recover some prestige by giving an overly large tip to the attendant accompanying me, but common sense prevails. So what if they think I'm a poor wretch unfit for their classy hotel. It's true, isn't it?

I give him a decent amount, the same as I gave to the porter at the place I chose myself. But that's not all. I ask: "Is the faucet water drinkable?" He probably knows I need to know this for my instant cappuccini and soups. Too bad.

"Oh yes," he says, "and it's very good."

I'm not hungry, but as soon as I'm alone I eat a slice of cheese and two cookies. I'll have to go back to the Writers' Union in the afternoon and hope that, once the excitement over the arrival of a Western traveler has passed, one of them feels like sitting down quietly with me and answering my questions. Even Ante Radek.

Ante Radek is not there. I refrain from asking after the morbid-smelling president, and instead approach a poetess sitting alone at one of the tables. She has a notebook on her knees and a pen in her hand, but she doesn't look like she's writing.

"May I ask you a few questions?"

"Of course. Please sit down." She slides the pen into her half-disheveled bun of grey hair. This seems to me an artistic gesture, well beyond anything one might see in nature. Perhaps it is with such gestures, and with her black dress and face so pale it looks dusted with flour, that the poor woman hopes to maintain her status in the category of poets, legitimizing herself for the small government stipend granted those so called. Her name is Lyuba Bogomila. Perhaps she once wrote a few good lines and now they just don't come to her anymore: at any rate, the pages of her notebook are blank, as far as I can tell, aside from the name written on the cover.

"It's about the information I was asking for this morning. Do be so kind as to give me a hand. You've all been so nice to me, you celebrated my arrival, but no one has told me anything yet. Your president walked me back to my hotel and the whole way he did nothing but talk about Italo Calvino. So just for starters: is Milos Jarco in town or is he away?"

"I believe he's out of the country. A few hours ago I heard the secretary say that to someone. To you, actually. Yes: didn't she tell you he was away?"

"I was hoping she was wrong. Someone told me he saw him this morning strolling on the Promenade. The hotel porter told me . . . I don't remember his name. He was the porter at my hotel."

"Don't you remember the name of your hotel?"

"I was referring to my first hotel . . . I've since been moved to the Esplanade."

I tell her about my transfer. She looks at me with an odd expression. "I understand," she says.

I don't understand what it is she understands. I press on with more questions. "Don't you have at least some anecdote," I ask, "some personal memory of him?"

"My dear, all I ever see of Milos Jarco is a brief glimpse now and then at official ceremonies, and that's it. He's a big shot, he doesn't mingle with old poetesses from the provinces."

"But I was referring to the past. To the time before he became famous."

"Oh, that time?" The poetess laughs slyly. "Before he became famous he was such a little shot that it was I who didn't mingle with him! That man went from nonexistence to world fame in a flash. Just think, when Milos Jarco first aroused the interest of the entire literary world—with his famous speech at the PEN Club conference at New York, as I'm sure you remember—well, the galleys to his first novel hadn't even been printed yet! He left here as a nobody—and I'm speaking literally, mind you: among us artists no one, not a soul, had ever heard of him—and returned as a celebrity. Never, not for a single moment of his life, has he been on the same level as I. Do you understand?"

This is the first I've heard of this famous speech at the New York conference. I'm not the type who always gets the latest news as it appears. I began to read the novels of Milos Jarco when he was already famous, playing no part myself in the rising of his star. But I would rather pretend I'm up on everything, and so I ask no questions.

"So not even your president knew him, before . . . before his speech at the PEN Club?"

"Him? Well . . . I suppose he might have." She seizes me by the arm and brings her face close to mine with a conspiratorial air. "But he's not reliable, that man. He's completely mad. He married a Circassian who must weigh four hundred pounds, and on moonlit nights he dances naked on the riverbank, like a rabbit in heat."

"With the Circassian woman?"

"No, she sits and watches. He brings her along in her wheelchair and wraps her in a blanket."

"But isn't he a high school teacher? That's what I read on his calling card. I always thought they were very careful to know the mental fitness of those who teach children."

"Bah. They let him teach the children, and what's worse, they even let him choose what poetry to publish in our review. They allow a dangerous madman to remain in a very sensitive position, believe me."

She presses her notebook lovingly to her breast. Something must be written inside there, after all. A rejected text, I would guess.

I stay a little longer at the Writers' Union, interviewing other people. I learn that novelist A is a homosexual, that historian B has plagiarized his monograph on Pugachov from beginning to end, and that poetess C brings letterhead paper home from the office, along with other stationery items. One novelist has been twice divorced; an elderly poet married a woman thirty years his junior who constantly disgraces him with her scandalous behavior. The secretary leads me into a small room, sliding along the corridor with a noiseless step.

"Lyuba Bogomila is finished," she says. "She hasn't written a decent line since the day she murdered her mother."

"I beg your pardon?"

"Three years ago. A huge woman: she must have weighed four hundred pounds."

"Was she by any chance Circassian?"

"Circassian? I don't think so. They lived together in a tiny apartment. The old woman was ill, and very fat, mostly. And Lyuba killed her. Probably used one of those poisons that leave no trace."

I try to get back to the subject.

"Can you tell me anything about the life of Milos Jarco before his famous speech at the PEN Club congress?"

"I didn't know him. Ask our president. He was there, in New York, on that occasion."

"Oh." So I will have to turn to none other than Voytek Miczan after all, despite the fact that I don't like his smell. "So he was in New York too."

"Yes. He accompanied our younger writers."

So there was a whole delegation. Good. Perhaps I can find what I need without having to go back inside the cold-storage room of the Writers' Union president. All I have to do is talk to any one of those who took part in the conference. "Tell me about these younger writers. Was there more than one?"

"Uh . . . I think so. With all the commotion surrounding the name of Milos Jarco, the participation of the others was a bit obscured. But I'm sure our president was there, in his capacity as official delegate, along with, I think, two or three promising young writers of ours."

"Couldn't you try to remember who they were?"

"I have no idea. That was seven or eight years ago. At the time I certainly wasn't interested in that sort of thing. I was in charge of bookkeeping at the tannery. I hadn't yet met Voycko."

"Voycko?"

"Voytek Miczan. Our president. One day he came to give a lecture to the workers. I was acting as hostess, serving refreshments and so on. During the concert that closed the proceedings he came and sat next to me."

I realize she is about to start confiding in me, perhaps on amorous matters.

"Thank you so much," I tell her. "I'll go and see if anyone else can help me."

Primum per delectationem temporalium antiquus hostis praetendit, nunc vero per pulchritudinem rerum temporalium homini blanditur ut decipiat.
—Hugonis de S. Victore, *De Claustro Animae,*
Liber I

First availing himself of the temporal pleasures, the ancient enemy lays his traps, then with the beauty of earthly things he entices man so as to deceive him.
—Hugh of Saint-Victor, *The Secrets of the Soul,*
Book I

•

ANTE RADEK HAS ARRIVED. He wanders through the meeting hall with the look of waiting for someone. Under his arm he is holding a class register with a pink cardboard cover. On the label is written: "Third Course—Comparative Literature (Professor Ante Radek)." When I walk up to him I realize he was waiting for me.

"I wanted to ring you to invite you for a stroll in the city, but you had already left the hotel."

I wonder how he knows what hotel I'm staying at. He probably called the flophouse whose name I can't remember.

"I'm staying at the Esplanade now, you know," I tell him. Perhaps I've used the wrong tone—an idiotic tone, as if I were bragging. Whatever the case, his face turns grim.

"Yes, of course." He lowers his eyes, nods without smiling. "I guess they treat you pretty well there. It's a luxury hotel."

The way he says "luxury hotel" is a whole program in itself. It reminds me of certain tirades of my Church Fathers—*De vanitate mundi, De aviditate, De bonis materialibus.* They're just a couple of words, and an imperceptible movement of the head, but they're enough to make me feel uneasy.

"I had chosen a different one," I am quick to explain. "I don't remember what it was called. A very modest little hotel, actually. And when I went back there they told me they'd had to move me because my room in fact was not available, and that all the rest were taken too. And so I ended up at the Esplanade, carried there almost bodily and without any increase in price, apparently. Rather unheard of, really. I'm not sure if I should be pleased with it or not. I wouldn't want them in the end to present me with some enormous bill, despite all their reassurances."

"That certainly will not happen," says Ante Radek. I get the feeling he knows the real reason behind my transfer, or that the fact itself, for him, in the light of I don't know what, has a precise significance. His gaze is a wall of reserve.

"What exactly is it you're looking for?"

"I've already told you. I want to do an article on Milos Jarco for a women's magazine—and to interview him, if possible. And if it's not possible I would like to interview other people who might give me a portrait of the 'unknown' Milos Jarco, from the period before his famous speech to the PEN Club."

"Why?"

"What?"

"Why go digging around in a gloomy period of no historical importance? Why search through banalities that have nothing to do with literature?"

He too is resistant, like all the rest. Nobody here wants to give me a straight answer. They all sound the way I must have sounded when it was they who were questioning me on contemporary Italian literature and I kept to generalities to mask my ignorance. But Milos Jarco is another matter. How is it possible that here, in his hometown—a small provincial city where everyone should know one another personally—so little is known about him? Might they not have some obscure reason of their own for discouraging me from my pursuits?

"I have to dig around because that's the way our women's magazines approach cultural matters. They don't give a damn about Milos Jarco the writer, they only want to know about the less famous aspects of Milos Jarco the celebrity. The trick is to reveal what no one else knows about a man whom everyone knows."

"I know what your press is like, women's as well as men's. Here it's different. Our magazines don't go looking for such rubbish. What nobody knows about an artist is not worth revealing. It's just idle chatter, gossip."

"But I'm not trying to do a scandal piece. I merely want to talk about his schoolmates, his first girlfriend. I have no bad intentions whatsoever."

There is a tireless, fanatical innocence in Ante Radek's clear eyes. His Slavic traits, which in his overall physiognomy are only vaguely hinted, suddenly become very pronounced; in the line of the lips, the angle between the cheekbone and the temple, his face is now the face of an entire people: ancient, wise, simple, holy. He doesn't like luxury hotels or frivolous magazines. Perhaps that is why his clothing is so exceedingly shabby: clearly Ante Radek has something to say against any form of indulgence in aestheticism and vanity. Now his little brown suit seems to me something more deliberate: it is the uniform of a moralist rather than merely the fruit of bad taste and penury. So when he was eyeing me this morning, it was not because he felt attracted to me. Probably his gaze, which didn't leave me for a second, contained nothing but disapproval: for my beige linen slacks, my raw silk blouse, my hundred-dollar dark glasses—a rare caprice—which I wear on my head, as if to keep my hair back. For my wretched department-store opulence, for the modest veneer of elegance I manage to put on with all the more difficulty as the sums I can allot for this purpose grow ever more negligible.

Never would I have thought I could feel uneasy for being too smartly dressed. I of all people. Imagine that. In any case I came here for a purpose, and I can't let myself be intimidated by some Savonarola of the East.

"Do you know who was in the delegation that took part in the famous PEN Club congress in New York?" I ask him. If the president of the Writers' Union is truly a madman who dances naked on moonlit nights, perhaps he could tell me amusing, unconventional things about Milos Jarco; but I don't like his smell, or the chill that emanates from him. And anyway, I'm sure the officialness of his position would prevail over the eccentricity of the man, with the result that from him—however bizarre he may be in his private life—I would obtain only canonical information rehashed by all the press offices of the world. I'm much better off looking for someone else to help me.

"There was no delegation. Officially, our country was not present at the conference. It was decided merely that two young writers would be brought to New York to observe the proceedings of the congress as spectators. We had a new minister of education at the time—who's still in office—who was convinced of the advantages of opening up our culture to exchanges with the West."

I gather that in his opinion nothing good, for his country, will come from this exchange. "I suppose you don't agree," I say to him.

He doesn't answer. "Shall we go out?" he says instead. "I'm through with classes for the day. We could go somewhere and talk, perhaps have a beer and a sandwich."

He takes me to a crowded, noisy bar. I can't figure out if he's courting me or studying me for his own mysterious reasons. I ask him who the other writer was that went to New York with Milos Jarco. His answer gets lost in the din.

It is almost impossible to talk. We shout at each other in monosyllables while waiting a long time for a waitress to come and take our orders. I wonder whether his strict moral code demands that he pay for my order, or if the imperative is to go Dutch in homage to the equality of the sexes. By this point, though I don't know Ante Radek enough to guess what rules govern his behavior, I am fairly certain that there always is some inflexible rule that must be examined before making any decision, however small. To avoid the risk of bankrupting him I order the least expensive sandwich, with salami and sauerkraut. I'm actually rather hungry, but I resolve to supplement my supper with some soup and cheese when I get back to the hotel. In the end each of us pays for himself, but by then it's too late to order something more inviting.

We step out into the dark little street and set off for the Esplanade.

"I didn't quite get the name of the other writer who was in New York with Milos Jarco," I say.

He stops, takes both of my hands in his and looks at me in the darkness. "You're very beautiful," he says. "I don't know what you're up to, but whatever it is, forget about it. Take my advice."

I am unable to respond. I don't understand what he's trying to say to me. I only know he said: "You're very beautiful." My hand remains in his as we resume walking in silence. We've come out from the little street and onto the Hapsburg boulevard, which is deserted. From time to time, a lone passerby sticks his head out from one of the side streets, like a weasel looking out from the grassy fringe of a country road. And like a weasel, he looks suspiciously to the right and left before deciding to shoot across the street like an arrow only to disappear immediately on the other side. The Promenade, bathed in moonlight, is all ours. From the double row of linden trees wafts a light, sweet fragrance.

We reach the Esplanade without saying another word. In front of the revolving door, Ante kisses my hand. "I am sorry to see you go into this place," he says. I look up to the stuccowork on the facade, to the gilded domes; I figure his eyes probably see a steamy, disgusting mountain of the demon's excrement. "You have no business with a place like this." Then he bows solemnly: "Thank you for the pleasant evening."

I cook up some thick pea soup in the mug called "His." I cut a slice of ewe's cheese and carry everything to the table by the window. I turn off all the lights in the room, except for the lamp with the eagle, and eat as I watch the deserted Hapsburg boulevard, the black trees and the white buildings in the moonlight.

It's quite true that I have no business with a place like this. I had already thought of that myself: not with pride, to tell the truth, but with a certain regret.

You never took me to such a fancy place, not even after you started making money. But perhaps you've since started treating yourself to something comparable, when traveling with your economist friend? I doubt it. At any rate, here I am, darling, and I made it here on my own.

"Do you see where I am?" I say out loud. My words sound strange to me. "Do you see where I am?" I repeat. Then again, in an even louder voice: "When young Melissa sweeps the room / I vow she dances with the broom."

I walk to the middle of the room, stand on a chair, and begin to speak out, clear and loud: "My name is Valentina Barbieri, Prini by marriage, separated pending divorce. I am thirty-one years old, am five feet four inches tall, and weigh one hundred twenty-five pounds. I have chestnut hair and green eyes. I have a degree in Slavic languages and literatures, and the only purpose for my trip to this city is to interview Milos Jarco—if that is possible—and to write a feature article on his childhood and adolescence."

I step down from the chair. This is lunacy, I tell myself. It doesn't make sense. The thought in my head cannot be true.

Immediately, however, I convince myself of the contrary. It must be true, I'm not mistaken: someone is listening to me.

The two possibilities stand side by side. On the one hand, I "sense" that my transfer to the Esplanade is strange, that it can be explained only by assuming that the purpose was to keep me under surveillance: the personnel in this hotel are probably all spies and the rooms all bugged with microphones. On the other hand, I can't bring myself to believe that an adventure so extraordinary could ever happen to me. How could it be? Good old common sense keeps telling me that these strange things aren't happening and that there is always a simple explanation for everything. But there is also that strange new lucidity, which cleared up my mind so suddenly, without my wanting it to . . . What I don't understand is whether, when Riccardo went away with the nameplate from my door, the part of me that suddenly saw everything clearly—the horror and absurdity jumping up from the fog like tumblers—set off for destinations of greater wisdom or toward madness. I certainly no longer find myself in the comfortable, middle-of-the-road position of common sense: but to which side am I rolling? I wish I knew.

The fact is that the instant I uttered those first words aloud I "sensed" I was not alone. And also: why did Ante Radek have such an impenetrable expression on his face when we were talking about my transfer to the Esplanade? Why did Lyuba Bogomila say "I understand" in that tone of voice?

But I have nothing to hide, except for the five hundred dollars in the jack, which are illegal only according to the Italian monetary restrictions, unless—as you, Mama, maintain—the law has already been changed.

"Put them in your purse, silly," you said. "Nobody will say a thing."

I decide to allow myself the luxury of telephoning Milan.

"Everything all right?" you ask.

"Everything's awful. They've put microphones in my bedroom."

A moment of silence. Then: "What?"

It's not the microphones that surprise you, it's that I could be so hysterical as to get such an absurd idea into my head.

I tell you about my day, from beginning to end. "It doesn't make sense, I realize that," I conclude. "And yet it's true."

"But tell me, who would ever decide to do such a senseless thing?"

"I don't know, Mama. Them."

"Them?"

Uttered by you, that lone syllable plunges the whole conversation into the realm of the ridiculous.

"I don't know what to tell you. Someone. Voytek Miczan, I guess. He wouldn't let me leave the headquarters of the Writers' Union this morning. He kept me there almost by force, using the reception as an excuse. It's pretty crazy, if you think about it. Why on earth should they decide to make such a fuss over an unknown woman who shows up asking them for a little information? If you ask me, as they were all standing around me toasting me with anisette, he was on the phone arranging my transfer."

"But why on earth?"

"How should I know! I'm a jilted woman with the most paltry alimony imaginable, a working woman who did ten years of drudgery with nothing left to show for it; I'm a devoted student of 'their' culture, literature and tongue; I understand very little of politics, but I'm certainly no enemy; I come full of good intentions to do an article on their best novelist: what the hell more do they want? Whose papers could be more in order than mine?"

"Exactly. So enjoy your vacation and stop getting strange ideas."

I hang up the phone. I take a shower. As I'm drying myself, I go back into the room; in the middle of the room, I let the bathrobe fall to the floor and, stark naked, I say aloud: "Go on to bed," I tell them. "I'm not receiving any more secret agents tonight."

Quod monstruosius est monstrum luxuria, quae in capite suo gerit faciem virginis et imaginem voluptatis, in medio capram foetosae libidinis, in fine lupam, depraedatione virtutis.

> —Alani de Insulis, *Summa de Arte Praedicatoria*,
> Caput V, "Contra Luxuriam"

Indeed lust is the most monstrous of monsters, for on top it has the face of a virgin and the image of voluptuousness, in the middle a goat of foul lechery, and at the bottom a she-wolf to prey on virtue.

> —Alan of the Islands, *Treatise on the Art of Preaching*, Chapter V, "Against Lust"

•

I COULD BE WRONG, but I don't think so. The thing in itself is almost certain, and I say "almost" only out of superstition: Ante Radek is interested in me. Ante Radek with his gentle, boyish face. With his eyes so blue and his skin so fair that even on his eyelids, temples, and the tips of his cheekbones there's a barely perceptible shade of periwinkle blue, as if that color were too intense to remain confined to the sphere of his irises. It doesn't seem possible, but he's interested in me. What I don't quite understand is why. I don't know if his intention is to court me, to help me, or to spy on me. Who can say with any assurance whether he wasn't the one who had me moved to the Esplanade? During my first visit to the Writers' Union I remember very well that he disappeared for a good while when the others were besieging me with their questions . . . Might it not have been he on the phone, busy giving orders, instead of Voytek Miczan? It may seem a crazy conjecture, but isn't everything a bit crazy in this country, starting with the fact that I've been here twenty-four hours without finding a single soul willing to tell me anything about Milos Jarco?

If I reexamine and compare my conversations with Voytek Miczan as he walked me back to the hotel, with Ante Radek at the bar, with Lyuba Bogomila and the other writers and poets at the headquarters of their Union, I cannot ignore the fact that there is something strange here, as though Milos Jarco had descended on this city one fine day like a meteorite from the cosmic void. As though nobody, in fact, knew anything about him.

And since this is not possible, it seems, rather, that there is a genuine conspiracy of silence surrounding his name. And this hypothesis raises new questions.

The first is: is it really true that Milos Jarco is not a dissident, that his relations with the authorities are as idyllic as they say? This double city, with its two chaotic hemispheres stitched together by that anachronistic Austro-Hungarian Promenade where nobody sets foot except to squirt quickly from one side to the other, also has a double reality, as I have already had occasion to note. I have listened to the toasts and the conventional discussions, but I have also heard the words whispered in my ear. What if the authorities' celebratory attitude toward Milos Jarco were only a facade to hide from the world's eyes a secret conflict between the mother country and her celebrated son? Might there not be some sort of nonaggression pact between the two, formed in the common interest, to strike a happy medium? Might it not be that Milos Jarco simply found the right combination of sincerity, self-censorship, irony, and prudence for winning success in the West without having to renounce the enjoyment of a semiprivileged position at home, that of a man under a sort of deluxe police surveillance?

If that is the case, I will have driven endless miles for nothing. I have all the teachers I need at home for the sort of things a person like that could teach me: how to steer a middle course, to move along with little swipes of the tail, getting the maximum without risking too much: I certainly didn't have to come all this way to learn *that*. These are not the values I expected to find embodied in Milos Jarco. There's a big difference—though I probably couldn't define it—between sublime equilibrium and compromise, isn't there?

I set out only a few days ago and have just arrived, and yet I feel as if I've been searching for a thousand years, since the beginning of time. Like a mythic hunter on the ever-fresh, ever-elusive trail of some legendary prey—a great white stag that will let nobody catch him. Maybe I'll snag a giant crab. Or maybe I'm chasing a ragdoll.

And then, aside from the risk of having made a trip for nothing, might I not end up creating trouble for myself by persistently asking questions about Milos Jarco?

Lastly, is it true they put me up at the Esplanade to check on me with their microphones, or am I merely losing my wits? That overwhelming lucidity that invaded my mind a few days prior to my departure is still there; the doubts I'm having are perhaps a last-ditch attempt to hang onto the blissful obtuseness of yesteryear, when everything seemed to fit so nicely inside the reasonable confines of common sense.

No beating around the bush: deep in my heart, I know perfectly well that Milos Jarco is a forbidden name, that having uttered it has rendered me suspect, and that the staff of the Esplanade has been instructed to report all my actions.

I know this, and yet the next second I tell myself I must be going mad. Then I ask myself if we have no choice but to choose between being mad and being blissful idiots.

I have thrown away the cheese and salami, which had gone bad. I go out to buy some cookies. As I'm walking about the city I try to find again the street my original hotel was on. It's too bad I can't remember the name of the place: maybe the porter or the reader of American novels could tell me who wanted me moved from there, and why. Either one might be inclined to tell the truth, as long as I questioned them separately. Everywhere in the world, as far as I know, when one speaks with someone tête-à-tête the tone changes somewhat. Here, however, the transformation is astounding.

I dive into the little streets on the right side of the Hapsburg boulevard and walk for a long time, without, however, managing to find the old hotel. Perhaps it was on the left side? I come out across from the aquarium, cross the Promenade, and begin to search on the other side. I get lost several times, despite the map, and only with great difficulty manage to find the way back to my street. Finally, I give up. I happen to be just a stone's throw from the Writers' Union; I can see the flag waving two blocks away. There's no point in going back there, however, since nobody will tell me anything. Anyway, it's almost one o'clock and everyone will have gone home.

I ask a passerby where I might find a bakery to buy cookies; as I approach the shop I see Voytek Miczan coming out with shopping bag in hand. He is pale and dressed in black, more sinister than ever. He doesn't see me. He enters the front door of a grey, three-story building.

I take his calling card out of my purse. As I imagined, that's where he lives. The man gives me the creeps, his smell repulses me, but obeying a sudden impulse, I follow behind him. With each passing minute it seems more and more urgent that I find Milos Jarco; never mind that I have to subject myself to talking with Voytek Miczan. Perhaps, within the walls of his own home, he won't feel the need to behave so mysteriously.

Here too there's an elevator, adorned with the customary sign: OUT OF ORDER. On the third floor, I find his name on the door. I ring the doorbell.

After a few moments of near-total silence I hear something move inside the apartment and approach the mahogany door. It sounds to me like an enormous, monstrous mass dragging itself laboriously across the floor, panting. Now it stands motionless, without speaking, a few inches away from me. I ring again. "What do you want?" says a voice.

"My name is Valentina Barbieri. I'm looking for Mr. Miczan."

A few more seconds pass, then the door opens. In the doorway stands only the president of the Writers' Union. And yet mixed with his usual refrigerator smell, I detect a sweet, heavy, musky scent in the air. If the Circassian exists, she must have been behind that door a moment ago.

I don't know what to say. I feel embarrassed, as if I had interrupted Voytek Miczan in the middle of some erotic pursuit. The shudder I feel is not so much one of fear, now, as of disgust. In that ugly apartment an atmosphere of lust seems to float in the air.

The smells of cold storage and oily perfume blend together in revolting fashion, suggesting every manner of obscene image to my mind—the ghostly light of the moon on the river, the horrific monument of flesh hoisted on her wheelchair and the grotesque, greenish nakedness of Professor Miczan, entranced in his Sabbath . . . I make a great effort not to turn around and bolt down the stairs; to overcome the impulse I tell myself it's neither right nor logical to consider the sexual fantasies of others—even of the likes of Voytek Miczan and his gigantic Circassian lady—incompatible with morality, decency, and hygiene, and not to look the same way at our own: the game of the photographer, or the mechanic . . . Remember? Do you do it with your economist friend too?

And then the Circassian woman might not even exist. Lyuba Bogomila could have invented the whole story. I haven't yet had a chance to verify whether or not any of the gossip raging in this town feeds on secret truths. They might all be fantasies, an enormous joke, a contest of lies in which everyone takes part. I hope that's not true, however; or not entirely true, at least. That's precisely why I rang

Voytek Miczan's doorbell: in the hope of finally managing, in a private encounter, to extract some tiny grain of truth regarding Milos Jarco, however embellished by hyperbole and assorted slander.

"I was on my way to the bakery," I tell him, "and I saw you go into your house. I took the liberty of disturbing you to ask if you could perhaps give me a minute of your time."

He keeps me standing in the stench of the windowless foyer. "Please," he says, "what can I do for you?"

I play my high card. After all, the secretary of the Writers' Union could be ill-informed. "I would like you to introduce me to Milos Jarco so I can interview him."

My strategy fails. "That's impossible. Milos Jarco is away. He won't be back before Christmas."

So it's true. Isn't it? I decide, while awaiting new developments, to take this as good news.

"Well then, the address of his family will do for now. As I said, I'm trying to write an article on his childhood and adolescence, mostly. Actually I don't even need him."

"He has no one. He was an only child, lost his father when just a baby. Then his mother died two years ago."

I aim a little lower. "Some schoolmates, then."

"I wouldn't know. But if you ask at the university, at the department of contemporary literature, you'll find all that's worth knowing."

"Thank you very much, but, you see, those are things I already know . . . , that everyone knows, and they don't concern the period I'm interested in. I'm looking for something a little more playful. I work . . . I would like to work for a women's magazine." And here I decide to strike my most touching chord: "I need to work. I collaborated with my husband for years, and now we're divorced and I have nothing to my name, officially speaking. I don't have a profession . . . In our country it's hard enough to find work when you're twenty, imagine when you're thirty . . ."

"I have no materials to give you here . . . I'll look around my office. We'll talk about it at the Writers' Union in a couple of days."

His face is no more encouraging than his smell, but I force myself to insist: "But I don't want any materials. Just tell me something you yourself remember . . . It was you, after all, who took him to New York to the PEN Club congress, wasn't it? I would like to know why you chose him, what he was like then, whether he was an ambitious young man, whether he believed in his talent, whether he was in love, whether before his success he was as attractive as he looks today in the photographs, or whether he was just a drab young man . . ."

He rests a frozen hand on my arm and pushes me out of his house. "You will be taken care of by the end of the week."

I am on the landing; down the narrow staircase the thud of the door still echoes. Why "you will be taken care of"? Why not "you will have what you need"? We are speaking his language, not mine, but I'm sure I've grasped the exact meaning of his statement. The words he said can only be translated as: "You will be taken care of." Am I supposed to take this as a threat? And why should I, anyway? What kind of wasps' nest am I poking at?

I go back to the hotel after buying a bag of cookies. They're not very good, but I eat almost half of them while searching the room for microphones. By now I'm positive they must be there. I'm not quite sure why, but I no longer ask myself. Maybe Milos Jarco is a spy for the Americans, for all I know. I don't care. Here I'm finally doing something on my own, and for whatever reason—perhaps because of my ineptitude or some politico-literary intrigue of which I know nothing— everyone is trying to trip me up.

Would it have been any different if you had come with me? In certain ways not in the least—I speak the language and you don't, that's already a point in my favor. Unless, perhaps, that's why . . . You would have gone to the Italian Consulate, to the Dante Institute . . .

I consult the telephone book: there is no Italian Consulate in this city, no Dante Institute, no Italian Cultural Institute. So you see, my dear, you would not, after all, have gotten any farther than I have.

I lie down on the bed. It had been months since I last thought of our playing photographer or mechanic... The heavy atmosphere of lechery I thought I sensed at Voytek Miczan's house brought back the memory.

Now I can tell you the truth: at first your little inventions seemed mostly silly to me. For example, when you first told me to sit at the desk as though nothing were happening and to act as though you weren't there.

"Go ahead and write," you said to me, "make some calls, play a game of solitaire, or do the crossword puzzle." What nonsense.

You spread a cloth over my knees, as with a paraplegic in a wheel-chair, and you dived down there armed with a flashlight and began to fiddle about like an old-time photographer under his black curtain. It is impossible to enumerate all the different sensations that were stirring inside me; the predominant one, however, was a sense of the ridiculous-ness of it all.

"What on earth are you doing down there!" I shouted. You kept at it a while longer while I laughed and squirmed, and then you popped back out all red in the face and furious, and pulled the cloth rudely off my knee.

"You're illiterate in eroticism," you said.

I suppose your new friend, on the other hand, got the hang of it at once, when it was her turn. She probably taught you a thing or two herself, I'm sure.

In any case, I caught on pretty fast myself. A few days later, when you introduced the game of the "mechanic"—making me sit down on a seatless chair without any panties on, with you lying down belly-up with your back on a cushion, like a mechanic on his dolly—I already knew how I was supposed to act. And when you wanted us to change places, I likewise knew how to play the part—you certainly can't deny that.

But although I had intuited the rules of the game and managed to play along without making any mistakes, I didn't understand the reason for these acrobatics, I didn't know what to make of them.

It took me years to understand, because we never discussed it. As far as I know, couples who take pleasure in little games of this sort—who take a creative approach to lovemaking—usually talk about it endlessly; they think up new refinements, taking their cues from the sorts of books that even Mama has, mixed in together with her cookbooks—and which are so similar to her cookbooks that it's easy to confuse them: *A Hundred Taoist Ways to Love Without Penetration, A Hundred Main Courses Without Meat, New Sex Every Night with the Same Partner, Making the Best of Your Leftovers.*

The two of us, on the other hand, never talked about it. Our sexual encounters were almost clandestine—as if we were keeping our love-making a secret from ourselves—totally separate from the rest of our lives. During the day I used to have trouble remembering I was your wife and not your secretary and housekeeper; and if I did happen to remember, it was never due to any husbandly attitude on your part but rather because I would realize you weren't paying me.

That is why, to understand you, I had to manage it alone, and it took me a long time. But in the end I did it. Don't think I'm as silly as I seem. You, my illustrious master of eroticism, not only like to leave the soul out of the act of love, but also—for safety's sake—the body as a whole. You only want to deal with a single anatomical part, or to surrender your single anatomical part for it to be taken care of, leaving "you" outside of the whole affair. And me too, of course. The two of us, outside of it all. That way we avoid embarrassing intimacies, emotional compromises. Who is that woman doing the crossword puzzle? I wouldn't know. I have nothing to do with her.

Is that how it is? It certainly is: I haven't the slightest doubt. And let me tell you, it's not some Oriental erotic game, but a devilish perversion, the worst I can possibly imagine.

So devilish, in fact, that when I understood its meaning I, too, began to like it. It simultaneously revolted me and aroused me. And you must have intuited this, for very soon thereafter you stopped desiring me. You were amused only so long as I didn't like the game and felt ashamed; then, no more. End of game and of everything else.

Here, from a geographical distance of two thousand miles—and a million light-years of some other distance I'm unable to define—I now can tell you that you're a filthy pig, good professor, and that your new sweetheart must be quite a slut herself and will not fail, I'm sure, to bring grist to your mill according to your merits.

*Patet ergo quantae amoenitatis locus ille fuit . . . qui fontibus et fluminibus irriguus,
arboribus omnis generis frondosus et nemorosus, fructo tam pulchro ad videndum quam
suavi ad vescendum refertus praedicatur.*
                              —Hugonis de S. Victore, *Dogmatica*, Pars II

It is well-known how delightful that place was . . . which, it is said, was watered
with springs and rivers, verdant and wooded with trees of every kind, rich in
fruits as beautiful to behold as they are sweet to the taste.
                              —Hugh of Saint-Victor, *Dogmatica*, Part II

•

ANTE RADEK'S PHONE CALL wakes me up at nine. He
stammers a little. "You . . . you weren't sleeping, I hope?"

"No," I say.

"For two hours now I've been dialing your number and hanging up
halfway through . . . I was afraid I would wake you up, or that you had
already gone out and I wouldn't find you there."

"Everything's fine," I reassure him. "I'm awake and I haven't gone out
yet."

I hear him swallow. "I have to teach until three," he says. "What
would you say to taking a walk, later, along the river? There's a place
there where one can rent a boat."

During the morning I register a few useless impressions of the city on my tape recorder. What on earth am I doing here? The less I manage to get done, the more convinced I become that I have to find Milos Jarco, at all costs. On the other hand, however, the more I insist, the vaguer are the answers I get, the thicker the smokescreen hiding him from me.

While waiting for the two days to pass so I can have another go at Voytek Miczan, hoping I'll be "taken care of," I have decided not even to bother going to the Writers' Union in the meantime. I'm better off probing Ante Radek through and through than wasting my energy questioning twenty people who have nothing to tell me.

Without much hope I pay a quick visit to Milos Jarco's publishers. There I get exactly what I expected: vague replies and an envelope full of stale news and articles I've already read.

I go back to the hotel, wash my hair, do a bit of laundry in the sink, and hang it up to dry in the bathroom. I decide to wear a skirt for our walk along the river, that way it will be easier to slip off my underthings and put on my bathing suit if we decide to go swimming. I run the iron quickly over the last of many skirts Federico has given me for my birthday, which look a lot like the ones you wear, Mama.

All of you are always thinking of what's best for me: for Riccardo what's best for me is for me to fade slightly out of the picture and take several steps back to make way for his new sweetheart—while remaining, however, discreetly in orbit around the original love nest to fulfill the tasks of slave, secretary, housekeeper, occasional lover, and emergency landlady in case of quarrels. For you, what's best for me is for me to tell Riccardo and every other man in the world to go to hell, and then go out and find unceasing success in some not very well-defined career. But what career, Mama? You have to tell me. What do you think I know how to do? You never set great hopes on Bohaboj Atanackovic, I hope. Perhaps you're confident I'll bring back a really good article on Milos Jarco. That's what I was hoping too, before coming here; but the fact is, Mama, nobody wants to help me. Worse yet, they look at me as if I were the secret agent of some foreign power looking for who knows what.

For Federico, however—and this is why he gives me gypsy skirts on every occasion—what's best for me is for me to become as much like you as possible. He has no doubt about it, and he does nothing to hide his certainty. When he sees me a little spruced up he says, "Well done, darling"—he says, "When you make yourself pretty you look just like your mother."

At one o'clock I go out for lunch to a sort of snack bar not far from the Esplanade, then I come back to rest, change my clothes and make myself up so that I'll look my best when Ante comes to fetch me. It's been years since I last spent more than ten minutes on making myself pretty. These odalisque-like preparations, executed with a solemn, meticulous ritualism, put me in an Olympian, neutral state of mind—as though my body were a precision instrument or a fine, well-oiled car, and I the most professional of racers about to get the very best possible performance out of it.

I sway my hips back and forth in front of the mirror.

Mama, I don't look like you at all. My hair is straight—as yours would be too, if not for your Afro perm—and I'm much thinner than you, even now that I've put on a few pounds. My eyes are the color that sympathetic friends and relatives like to call green, but which in reality is a light hazel, without the witchlike glint that yours have. My eyelashes, however, are long, dark and silky, and my skin has acquired a subtle glow during this trip: a very light, rosy shadow on the cheek-bones.

I am the way I am, but sometimes—like now—I can look at my reflection with a certain satisfaction.

Ante arrives on time. He has the porter ring me from the lobby. When I go down I find him waiting for me on the outside staircase.

"About a quarter mile from here we can catch a bus that will take us to the wharf," he says. He's dressed the same as the other day; in a plastic bag he has his bathing suit and towel.

"We can take my car," I tell him. We go down to the garage. I ask him if he wants to drive. "I don't know how," he says.

I take him aboard and, raising his arm as if to dress a child, I strap the seat belt around him, which is obligatory here. I shut his door, turn on the radio. Sitting like this beside Ante, who is such a stranger to it all, makes me feel very much at home inside my little car. Whatever way you look at it, this little cubicle of space is my element—personally, because it belongs to me and I know how to control it; and ethnically, because the country I come from, Italy, is the land of total motorization, where one is born with four wheels. Ante is only a guest here, and not the most relaxed guest at that.

I drive down the boulevard at full speed, amusing myself by shocking him. His pale eyes are large and round, and somewhat deep set. His dominant trait is a gentle concavity—eyes, cheeks, the slight depression at the shoulder joints, the V-shaped void between waist and ribs. It's a delicate thinness, tender and defenseless. His points of strength, of masculinity—the broad shoulders, the golden shadow of beard—have something incongruous about them that makes one's heart ache. This mixture of amazement and sadness must be what mothers feel when they finally realize their boys have become men.

I keep looking over at him as I fly through his city. It's the first time since you left me that I find myself in a situation that has a chance to evolve into an amorous adventure. I am touched to be with this handsome, mild-mannered poet so different from you, Riccardo. Yes, different. Very different. He doesn't make me feel uneasy, do you know what I mean? I don't have to keep asking myself what I should say or do to please him. On the contrary. There is something in his way of looking at things, of pronouncing every word, of performing each act, which awakens the desire in me to take care of him and comfort him. It's the same yearning that comes over me when I see little children from my window in the morning, who are on their way to school and who seem to me—from the way they quicken their pace, or the way they hold their satchels—like good children. I see them walk by in such a hurry and I realize that their primordial innocence is still intact, that they help their mothers to clear the table and copy their handwriting assignment in their notebooks with every ounce of energy and enthusiasm they have. . . . Is there any way I can look at these young things without feeling my heart grow heavy with . . . I don't know with what. Maybe with a sense of guilt, of shame, as if I had some tremendous debt to them that I never intended to settle . . . What does it mean? Oh, *you*, Riccardo, would be the last person ever to understand an emotion of this sort. "The little children touch your heart because it's the most normal thing in the world, and that guy appeals to you because he's a big handsome blond with blue eyes." That's what you would say.

"You're a very courageous woman," observes Ante. "When I first saw you come into our offices looking so young and vulnerable, I should never have thought you had come all this way by yourself, driving all those miles."

As we are racing down the Promenade, once again I can't help but notice that it's completely deserted. Or rather, many people are crossing it, but none are walking along it. The city's life goes on to the right or to the left of the Hapsburg boulevard which, for its own part, acts as a virtual demarcation line rather than as a real element of the topography.

When we reach the river we cross the bridge, then drive along it upstream for a few minutes, leaving the tannery behind us. We stop the car in the square in front of an ugly building that houses a snack bar, a boat depot, and an enormous depository of deck chairs for rent. Since it's a weekday, there are very few people. We buy two beers and ham sandwiches and then request from the attendant a light, slender boat, almost a canoe, its wood painted sky blue.

Ante rows without effort; the boat skims along the water's surface and soon we are far from the bank.

Here, upstream from the tannery, the water is a limpid blue. There are many islets on the river. We choose one of the smallest: round, overgrown with beech and birch trees in the center and fringed all round with a ring of white pebbles.

We tie the boat up and walk into the wooded area until we reach a small, sheltered clearing covered with sand.

"You can change here if you want, no one will see you," says Ante. He walks off as I'm putting on my bathing suit, and when we meet back up on the islet's shore he already has his bathing shorts on. His clothes are hung in orderly fashion from the branches of a shrub; the towel is spread out in the sun with a rock on each of its four corners to keep the wind from blowing it away.

Ante has the firm flesh of his age but is not particularly muscular. I wish I could touch his chest, so tenderly gaunt, run my fingers along the ribs as if to count them, lower my hand into hollow triangle above his navel, feel the softness of the little golden hairs.

"Are you sensitive to cold?"

"Not really." I'm actually extremely sensitive to it, but I've decided I'm going to have a swim. We shall dive in together, keep each other from falling as we walk on the slippery rocks, dry each other's back when we come out. He will follow my lead, in his own way: I've already understood that I will have to be the one to initiate the seduction— perhaps because he's younger than I, or because I come from the West, or because I know how to drive a car.

I hold out my hand to him. "Come," I say to him. We enter the water, which is freezing cold and immediately deep. I swim a few strokes and then surrender myself to the river's current, which takes me back to the island. "Let's try to go as far as that sand bar," I say to him, "then float back to shore."

We swim hard against the current for about thirty yards; Ante gets there first and waits for me, hanging onto the branch of a birch tree sticking out of the water. "Come on," he says, holding his hand out to me as I swim my last few strokes. When I reach him, he seizes me by the waist. I let myself be held up, my body supported by his, swaying along with his to the rhythm of a small whirlpool. As I regain my breath I feel an intense heat running through my veins in reaction to the cold.

"Shall we go?"

"Let's go."

His hand lets go of the branch and, rolling in each other's arms from one eddy to the next, we let the current cradle us back to our island.

It's like a long waltz full of spirit and abandon, which ends sweetly on the white, warm pebbles. As he is drying me I untie my bathing suit, letting it fall to the ground: first the bra, then the two little ribbons holding up the bottom.

It's not my style, to make the first move like this. Never in my life have I dared do anything of the sort. Here, however, everything is different—or better yet, here, *I* am different. Or is this six-foot-three little boy the thing that's truly different, previously unknown? As I was driving him in the Volkswagen down the Promenade I already felt as if I were carrying him off in the saddle of the Hippogriff. I felt that he was mine—my quarry, my prisoner, my victim, my puppy. The game is still going on now, and even I don't know if it's a sweet or bitter game—but it certainly is new for me, as is the excitement I feel rising inside me in warm, slow waves. I try to keep it under control, to avoid making a mistake and frightening him. I must be careful. This is a role whose rules I don't know yet. I do like it, though. His wet bathing suit sticks to his skin as I labor to pull it down.

Now I let him take over and follow his lead, then I again take the lead, and again follow him in his sweet awkwardness. Then no one commands or obeys any longer, and I think again of a dance, of the rhythmic accord of a pas de deux. Then I stop thinking altogether.

Afterward, I turn onto one side, elbow resting on the sand, head resting in my hand. I feel strong. Virile. He is lying on his back, spent. His blond curls are tousled and the slight blue shadow under his eyes has grown more intense.

"Come on," I say to him, "tell me a little about Milos Jarco."

7

Unum tamen scio, quia nullus est nostrum, qui non momentis omnibus elaboret, ut plus habeat, quam habebat.

—Sancti Zenonis, *Tractatus III, De Justitia, 37*

I know only one thing, that there is not one of us who by every means does not do all he can to have more than he has.

—Saint Zeno, *Treatise III, On Justice, 37*

●

THEY'VE BEEN SNOOPING around in my things. The tape-recorder case has been put back in place and fastened with its little spring hook, which I haven't used since the time when I couldn't open it up and had to resort to using a screwdriver.

Not even on the island, after making love, did Ante Radek want to talk to me about Milos Jarco. "All I know about him is what everyone else knows," he said. A lie, no doubt.

By now I am positive I have stumbled onto a taboo subject. Unless they have mistaken me for someone else. Did the secret services perhaps warn of the arrival of some Western spy in this remote city, and now the people here have got it into their heads that I'm that person? Have I, without knowing it, walked into a Gogol comedy? It must be one or the other. I can't imagine any other explanation—at least as long as I keep seeing things in the light of this dreadful clairvoyance, which hasn't faded during my trip, not even in the paradise of the islet on the river, when I was in Ante's arms. That familiar fog that used to round off the corners and allow me to fit everything within the confines of common sense is showing no signs of coming back. And yet—and this is the most astonishing aspect of my new way of seeing things—I remember how it used to be. When I observe and understand a phenomenon—naked, unvarnished, and unacceptable as it now appears—I also know how I would have perceived it a month ago. I remember the unconscious adjustments, the mental censorings, the banalizations. I remember the procedure and keep it tucked away, like some primitive language now unusable, or like an old wood stove in a condominium in the city, or a wicker cradle in a home without children.

It's there, in the attic, ready for my use. I can even—and sometimes do—find answers according to the old procedure, like someone who decides to cook a roast on the old kitchen range. And then everything finds a quick and very simple explanation, and I know that all further excogitations are just nonsense or worse. That one must be careful not to get carried away. That madness lies in wait for those who abandon themselves to mad thoughts.

I pour two capfuls of lemon balm bubble bath into the tub, let the hot water run a while and then immerse myself voluptuously in it. In spite of everything, it is a happy moment, because my mind is like a garden full of many different trees. In its far reaches, where thoughts of Italy roam, this is not so. Back there, there's still that one malignant weed devouring everything, leaving room for nothing else: you—you with your brass nameplate that you took away from me, with the fur coat you gave to that slut, with all the years you squeezed out of my life, with the paltry love you felt for me, with the slightly greater love—though not much—I felt for you, and mostly with that overwhelming, desperate love that sprang up out of spite at the very moment you went away. In that remote region, you're still the main and only character.

The closest thoughts, however, today's thoughts, afford me an enchanting variety. Ante Radek with his fine body, his tireless candor, his frighteningly gentle eyes: that's one thing. But there's also, entirely unrelated to my dawning emotions, the thrill of the hunt, the desire to track down Milos Jarco—wherever he might be hiding—at all costs. And also, a little farther away—this, too, distinct from the rest, destined to blossom on its own terrain—an ever so slight, electrifying shudder of fear. Because the atmosphere in which my investigations are taking place is truly a strange one. And lastly, my curiosity about this country so different from mine, about these two shabby, incomprehensible half-cities held together as if by a zipper by the Hapsburg boulevard, relic of a lost, incongruous world.

Tell the truth, Riccardo: is this what it's like to be a man? Is this the difference? I feel as if I've just made a fundamental discovery, because the point is right there, in the old "having so many things on one's mind," as you men like to put it, so that each thing, in the end, lessens the importance of all the others.

Women of my sort, in general, have only one thing at a time on their minds, and this is our downfall.

Isn't it funny that I had to drive two thousand miles, seduce a poet, get myself perhaps into trouble with Iron Curtain counterespionage, and immerse myself in a lemon balm bubble bath just to experience at last the very sensation that you, Mama, along with your friends, have already known for twenty years? Until now I had never had even the vaguest sense of it, perhaps because of a strange sort of rebounding effect that made me, while growing up in the bosom of the movement, the silliest of my generation.

You, Mama, embraced everything wholesale: feminism, astrology, yoga, psychoanalysis, herbalism, politics, acupuncture, homeopathy,

Hermann Hesse, *Kama Sutra*, macrobiotics, Chinese cooking. It's a mixed bag that has done you good; in me, however, some sort of blockage seems to have held everything up. That orgy of unconventionality must have set me back half a century.

But I won't ruminate too much on it: that would be stupid, old-fashioned, inconsistent with the beauty of my egotistical body luxuriating in the foam, inconsistent with this self-indulgence in my new thoughts and the scented warmth of my lemon balm bath.

It's nice to feel oneself on the other side, for once. Who was that mythological character . . . Tiresias the seer? He experienced both: being a man and being a woman. Afterward he said he found it much better being a man. I believe him. I find it much better too. I lift a foot out of the water and contemplate it. It's slender, sinuous, pink. A few tufts of white lather cling to it, contrasting with the red-painted toenails.

As we were eating our sandwiches in the clearing on the island, Ante said: "Cruelty is a necessary evil."

I had merely suggested that next time we meet in my fine double bed at the Esplanade instead of continuing to make love in the bushes. What did he mean? Was it an answer to my question? And what did it have to do with anything, what was the connection? No doubt his words were very high in moral content. For him, that is; for the way his conscience functions—a conscience which you, Mama, would call fanatical. But you know, I'm beginning to realize that of course one can be inoffensive and good-natured without being fanatical, but can one be saintly? You, Mama, are living proof of this. You are never shocked by anything, you never condemn anything. "Difference" is your passion. "Why not?" is your favorite expression. Or: "What do *we* know?" What do we know about why so-and-so killed his grandmother, why ten thousand voters elected a porn queen to parliament, why the dirty old man seduced his underage sister-in-law? Everything has its own justification—which you, of course, don't try to grasp but merely presume. It's all life. And yet despite your wonderful 360-degree openness, when I tell you my worries and nightmares you don't make the slightest effort to understand me. You get distracted after a few seconds. "You shouldn't eat tuna in the evening," you say. What? With all that you've read on dreams, from dream-books to Freud?

There's no point in mentioning that in your outmoded open-mindedness you're actually happy I'm separated. "It wasn't working," you say, "it's better this way." This also made me uneasy, even then, before my flash of lucidity. Now I can see it even more clearly, and it makes me feel very disappointed. I'm disappointed that you refused to fulfill your role. It was a conventional, old-fashioned role—after all, now and then, we have to steel ourselves and accept even such roles. You should have done it, however stupid it might seem to you, if you wanted to help me as I wished. I was the protagonist of the drama, was I not? Well then you should have intuited my desires and acted accordingly. I wish you had defended my marriage with tooth and nail. Not only that: you should have reproached me too. Never mind that the fault lay entirely with Riccardo; you should have accused me of not being understanding, of having neglected something: makeup, hair, cooking—I don't know.

As long as there was something to be gained, of course. Once everything had gone to the dogs, things had to change, that was clear. And from that moment on you should have stood by me fiercely, body and soul. You should have banished Riccardo from your sight. Instead—it's unbelievable but it's so you—you rejoiced when we split up and now you're great friends with Riccardo, whereas you didn't even like him before.

You say: "I didn't like the way he treated you. But as a man he's very charming."

Oh really. You didn't like the way he treated me but you can think of nothing to criticize in the way he treated me. Fine, as long as you can appreciate such subtleties of grammar.

You say: "Look at you: when you were married you didn't wear your wedding ring and now, all of a sudden, you parade it like a flag. How did it ever occur to you to start wearing your wedding ring on the very day of your separation? Can you tell me that? You're simply mad, Valentina. You just want to feel bad, if you ask me."

Come on. That's another matter, Mama.

You say: "Well surely you can admit it's a little strange."

So it's strange. I pull my hand out of the foam and look at the little gold ring. Your problem, Mama—or rather your good fortune—is that you don't even know what it means to feel bad. You talk about it the same way you talk about politics. From hearsay. When you've got it right under your nose, my feeling bad, that is, you don't see it, you don't recognize it. "It must have been the tuna in the evening," you say. "I'm always telling you, you have to watch what you eat, especially in the evening."

And that's that. I guess you just can't conceive of any other kind of malaise.

But I try to explain to you that the tuna has nothing to do with it. "But of course it does, dear," you say, already distracted, tired of listening to me. "You had a nightmare. It happens to everybody."

Now I don't even try any more to repeat the same things to you, for the hundredth time, but I really wish you would get it into your head that it was not a nightmare. Not by a long shot. First of all, I was awake. In bed with the light off, but awake. And there was nothing terribly frightening about what I was thinking at the moment. It wasn't even something I cared very much about. It was just a kind of lazy thought, the kind that come into your head and start to swirl around as you're about to fall asleep. I was thinking—believe it or not—of contemporary French writers. You can imagine how much I care about that. You know me: literature holds no great interest for me, as a rule. But it so happened that before going to bed, running through the circuit of channels with the remote control, I ended up at Antenne 2, which was broadcasting

Apostrophes. That was why I had that thought on my mind. I was telling myself: Damn, I'm totally out of touch with all this, I don't even recognize the names of the writers they've mentioned. I should read more, I thought—without really believing it, though: the way one says, for example, I should exercise more, I should keep a diary, and so on. You know how I am. And so, as I was lazily fantasizing about this, suddenly another thought caught hold of me: but I haven't even finished reading Stendhal, or Proust for that matter!

It was like an avalanche. Something that came crashing down on me, taking my breath away, throwing me into a panic that I can't even describe to you. A horrible feeling of vertigo, like being surrounded by an immense void and yet at the same time a feeling of suffocation, as if the darkness were closing in on me or my body were becoming intolerably tight, a prison of flesh with no doors or windows. And this terrible panic was progressive, it fed on itself. I said to myself: now, at least, I can actually turn on the light, go drink a glass of water . . . but what if the same thing were to happen to me when I was old or sick or for whatever reason unable to do anything to break the circle . . . ? And so I turned on the light, got up and drank a glass of water, but it didn't do any good, because it may have dissipated my present terror, but it didn't do anything for my hypothetical terror . . . And so the whole thing grew into this horrific logical paradox that cut across time, replacing fear with the fear of fear and making the return to normality purely hypothetical and the duration of the panic frightfully present. How can you say it was the tuna? And how can you call it a nightmare?

On top of all that, what happened to me lacked the essential characteristic of a nightmare, since my mind, before surrendering to panic, didn't even have the decency to pass through a metaphorical image of the terrifying vision—a werewolf, a giant spider, the living dead, Jack the Ripper, what have you. It just pulled it out of nowhere, out of a thought that was of no importance to me whatsoever . . . It didn't even take the trouble to think up a justification, as though it didn't care any more whether it was reliable or not . . . How can you not understand? I felt madness just a step away from me, and it wasn't the tuna, believe me.

You say: "Read then, if that's what you want so much. Read all of Stendhal and all of Proust, if that will make you feel better. Who's preventing you?"

Oh Mama. All that sage advice. And valerian. "It's totally natural, nothing chemical. It also comes in pills, but the tea is much better. With a teaspoon of honey." And the yoga exercises. And acupuncture. And, of course, the scientific explanation for it all: "It's only natural: you're a Sagittarius." Oh Mama. You're a really big help, no doubt about it.

"Why do you say that cruelty is a necessary evil?" I asked him.

"Because justice is unnatural," he replied. He was looking at me with those clear, clear eyes, his elbow leaning on the white sand, his muscles and ribs gently showing through the skin of his smooth, hairless chest.

"And is that why you don't want to come make love at the Esplanade?"

He gave me a kiss and lay down on his back without speaking, a hint of a smile at the corners of his mouth, his gaze out of focus, like a saint listening to his voices.

I let him be for a few moments, then began again to insist: "But really, why don't you want to come to the Esplanade? It would be so much more convenient. I know you don't like it, but you know, the world is full of monuments to injustice, large and small. You can't avoid them all. Why aren't you a little more flexible?"

He refocused his eyes and turned them toward me. "I'm too ignorant to be flexible," he declared. Then he smiled softly and shrugged his shoulders. "Do you know what original sin is?"

"What do you mean?"

"The real original sin of humanity, do you know what it is?"

"Sex, I guess."

"The original sin is to want more than it is right to want. Make a mountain with all the possessions one can possibly own in the world—all the pearls and diamonds, all the Japanese motorcycles, all the wool overcoats, all the potfuls of goulash, all the transistor radios: everything. Then count all the human beings that exist on the earth and divide up so much for each with the precision of a chemist: that's what's right and just. All the rest is unjust. It's very simple, everyone understands it, everyone knows it's true. It's pointless to circle around it with philosophical or political theories: even an idiot can see it, with the naked eye. The education of a seven-year-old is enough to make one see it . . . To throw more into it, to build a theory on something so obvious, is already suspect. It only helps to mask the simple truth. It helps to justify a life not consistent with this simple truth. It helps to create loopholes. It helps us to use truth as a weapon to bully people. It helps us to be flexible, as you put it. I'm suspicious of people who indulge in subtle arguments."

"Everyone indulges in subtle arguments," I said. "We're all so damned intelligent."

"Intelligent and dishonest. If someone's not scheming to cheat you he can very well afford the luxury of being simple. Things *are* simple. There is one evil that is the cornerstone on which all other evils rest, and it is greed. No one is immune to it. If someone is more fortunate, more cunning and more active, he manages to accumulate more than another: but what does it mean? The one who couldn't manage it is not a better man. Can one save one's soul by merely being unlucky, inept and lazy? Everybody always tends to think of riches greater than theirs as shamefully excessive, but do you really believe they would refuse to increase their possessions if they could? Therefore, yes, you are right: there are monuments to injustice, big and small, everywhere you look. It's true: the Esplanade is loathsome to me because of all the gilded spires, the lackeys in livery, the Oriental rugs . . . because it so arrogantly represents the happiness of having more than others have. But I'm also well aware that greed is not only there. It's in every man: in those who succeed in satisfying it as well as in those who can't. Failure doesn't absolve anyone."

"So what can you do about it? If it's nature that forces us to be this way, why do you get so upset?"

"If nature made us this way we must accept the corollary that justice can only be imposed by force. This is why I say that cruelty is a necessary evil."

Hear that, Mama? He is for punishing those who stray. A far cry from your "Why not?"! He's an atheist, but he talks like a seventeenth-century Jesuit. He has borrowed the vocabulary of religion because he says it's the most efficient, as well as the simplest, and he wants to use only simple words.

I asked him if he was a big cheese in the party and he opened his eyes wide and said: "Me? No, I don't count for anything. I haven't even read Marx. What do I need him for anyway? I'm more Marxist than he. I'm incapable of discussing such matters with my comrades: I don't know the terminology and I'm not interested in learning it."

At any rate, I've convinced him to come to the Esplanade tomorrow evening. He will be busy the whole day taking his students to see the city's factories. I will go to the department of contemporary literature at the university to see if I can find something out about this elusive Milos Jarco. Then I'll go and wait for him downstairs at the bar amid gilt ornaments, mirrors and velvet against a background of gypsy orchestra and jets of water in a salmon-colored fountain.

8

Vetas me irasci, vetas cupere, vetas libidine commoveri, vetas dolorem, vetas mortem timere: sed hoc adeo contra naturam est, ut his affectibus animalia universa subjecta sint.

—Lactantii, *De Vera Sapientia et Religione,* Caput XXIII

You forbid me to be angry, you forbid me to desire, you forbid me to be troubled by lust, you forbid me to fear pain and death: but this is so contrary to nature that all living beings are prey to these emotions.

—Lactantius, *On True Wisdom and Religion,* Chapter XXIII

•

I'M NOT GOING TO go to the department of contemporary literature at the university after all. If it's true that there's a conspiracy of silence around the name of Milos Jarco, they'll be more tight-lipped there than anywhere else. The fact is that the more I'm convinced that I *have to* make some sort of contact with Milos Jarco—to meet him or at least find out a little more about him—the more reluctant I am to utter his name. It makes me feel uneasy, as if I were committing some serious breach of etiquette. Is it possible this is a false impression that

I've made up myself? Why would I do that? To convince myself that without Riccardo I can't do anything right?

I keep thinking that if I could only find the old hotel, I'd be all right—as if it were some thread I could grab onto and methodically unwind, starting from the day of my arrival, when everything seemed so clear. I can't even remember if it was on the right or left side of the city. Actually, my memory is even more confused than that: I recall very well that the little hotel was on the right side, but at some point I seem to have changed my point of view, the base from which one's sense of right and left originates.

The Anglo-Saxons always reason in terms of cardinal points: north, south, east, west—rather definitive concepts, at least as long as one is on the planet. Good for them. I—like a good Italian on fairly unfamiliar terms with nature and her immutable laws—think in more relative terms: above, below, right, left. I considered the hotel as being on the right side of the city, but the question is whether at the moment in which I was forming this opinion I conceived of the Hapsburg boulevard as a river running downhill or as a flight of steps leading up to a temple—the temple being, of course, the thermal bath establishment with its columns, tympanum, and copper dome—since, to determine the right and left hand side of a river, I should have stood—as dictated by geography—with my back to the source. The beginning above, the end below, and hence the names of the two sides. But a staircase . . . Is that not something made to be ascended? Descending is nothing more than a return, right? I definitely remember that at a certain point, the boulevard dividing the city in two seemed to me very much like a staircase leading majestically up to the thermal baths, halfway up the hill; and if at that moment I had wanted to get my bearings in order to name the four directions, I doubtless would have reversed the perspective: the beginning would have become the end, the end the beginning, the right left and the left right.

I've got to find that hotel, wherever it may be.

It is six o'clock in the evening. I have a couple hours left before it gets dark.

I wander a long time around the city, remaining on the right side—so to speak. The side that would be the right one if I decided to see the boulevard as a river. It's more rational to conduct a methodical carpet-search over half the city than to hop and skip from one area to another and risk retracing my steps and leaving entire zones unexplored. Of course, if the hotel is on the other side, I could wander these streets for a thousand years without ever finding it . . .

It's mostly the boy, the reader of American novels, that I would like to find. When I think back on him I get a feeling of familiarity, and I know exactly why: he looked just like the boys back home: jeans, sneakers, white T-shirt. He's not foreign, he doesn't make me feel uneasy. With him more than anyone, I could commit what seems to be the worst possible blunder—that is, utter the fateful name—and everything would be all right. I would be more relaxed with him. I wouldn't have that unpleasant feeling of being always on the verge of saying or doing something uncalled for. I could drop my guard, momentarily forget the fact that here every little law—let alone the cornerstone law that holds the whole thing up—is the opposite of those that I know and obey at home.

I could forget all that because he played no part in instituting that law, nor in upholding it. He found it ready-made and well entrenched. Ante did too, for that matter. But unlike Ante, he—perhaps because he belongs to another generation—he seems to have no enthusiasm for it at all. Just look at how he dresses.

I am certain that the Western world, seen from this secluded town, must be like an infinitely distant but very bright star endowed with a relentless radiance that arrives all the way here from the formidable relay stations positioned in the bends in the border line, where that other reality forces its way into this one, making it possible for rock videos, *Dynasty*, and *M*A*S*H* to be seen everywhere. It is a radiance so powerful that clearly nobody can view it with a neutral mind. For Ante it is a poison polluting the atmosphere; but that boy surely sees it as the reflection of a magical world that for him is irresistibly seductive.

"Could you tell me why they moved me to another hotel?" I would ask the boy in jeans. "Could you tell me the real reason?" I could even slip him a few dollars. I don't think he would object to accepting them.

I walk and walk. Ante said he would come at nine, after supper. I have plenty of time, but I realize I'm wasting it. There's no trace of the hotel anywhere; it must be on the other side of the city.

Now there's no more asphalt: the muddy street I'm on is suddenly interrupted by a deep ditch. On the other side, atop a steep incline ravaged by bulldozers, rises a forest of grey buildings adorned with hanging laundry. A sign indicates this as the Yuri Gagarin quarter. The cosmonaut's name reawakens something in my memory: I search in my purse through the calling cards I was given after the party at the Writers' Union. I was right: Lyuba Bogomila lives here, at street 37, number 5, apartment 18.

Just ahead there is a little bridge of planks for crossing the ditch. I find the poetess's house: the elevator has the customary sign, but here there's a service elevator that actually works. I take it to the fifth floor.

Lyuba Bogomila is on her way out of her apartment. "I need to talk to you," I tell her. She shuts the door with a thud and leans her back against it.

"Not here at my place," she says. She looks at me straight in the eye, swallows and speaks as though making an inhuman effort to be sincere. "I don't want you to see my home. I can't . . . You have no idea . . ."

"Allow me to invite you for coffee somewhere," I propose.

"I was on my way to the cemetery . . . I like to go there in the early evening. It's a twenty-minute tram ride from here. Why don't you come with me? It's the most beautiful spot in the city."

We descend the incline together, and head in the opposite direction from the ditch. In the distance the road becomes paved again; the tram stops two blocks farther down.

"Please allow me to pay for you," says Lyuba.

"But why . . . ?"

"Please, it's my pleasure."

She buys two tickets from the ticket man and hands me one with a gracious gesture and a big smile, as when giving a gift. Maybe since she can't entertain me at her home, she is happy, at least, to have me as her guest on the tram.

"Thank you, you're very kind."

We leave the city, proceed on for a few miles across a grassy plain. The tram stops—we've reached the terminus—in front of a small, doorless shed containing various gardening tools. Lyuba takes a watering can and a small hoe. Five or six other people who got off with us equip themselves in similar fashion. An equal number of other people exit the cemetery, return the instruments they've just used and get on the tram, which immediately sets out again and takes them back to the city. In crossing paths they all exchange greetings and smiles.

In the great silence that descends on us after the tram has pulled away, the polite phrases still echo with a pleasantly antiquated sound.

Passing through a narrow opening in a well-pruned yew hedge, we enter the most amazing garden I have ever seen. Each grave is a flowerbed of incredible beauty: three feet by six feet densely covered with flowers. They are carpets, monochrome or polychrome, with geometric designs or jumbles of colors, formed by a compact surface of corollas rising just above the ground or by swollen cushions of flowering vines.

Lyuba fills the watering can at the fountain that stands at the center of the cemetery, then she stops in front of a cascade of blue flowers. At one end of the grave an invisible support holds the plants up so that they frame a photo of the deceased, about three feet above the ground;

from there the shoots descend gracefully down to the feet of the tomb. With her hand Lyuba pats the earth. "It's thirsty," she says.

Under the image of a young man with moustaches is a Hungarian name and the dates 1911–1941.

"Was he your husband?" I ask.

"No," she says. "My husband is buried a long way from here. I have no loved ones in this place. This one, however, is my favorite. They would be the same age if they were alive today. This boy and my Dušan, that is."

She waters the blue flowers, going back twice to refill the can. At another grave she pulls up a few plants now long past their flowering and replaces them with others she has brought along in her purse, wrapped in a damp page of newspaper.

"Now we can sit down a little," she says.

We walk to one of the wooden benches along the length of the hedge.

"It's very beautiful here," I say to her.

"Yes, beauty has fled to the cemeteries. Except, of course, for the great public buildings in the capital, and even a few here . . . Those buildings—even if they're not in step with the architectural fashions of the West—contain so much marble and granite and stained glass that they can't help but be beautiful. But the rest . . . Look around, when you're in town. It's hopeless: everything that's assigned to individuals is shabby, grey, ragged. The ancient pact between man and things is no longer in force—do you know what I mean? We don't give a damn about it anymore. We won't paint a wall, put a plant on the balcony, embroider a curtain. And it's not a question of money. We once had the custom of cutting out strips of paper using the same technique used to make strings of paper dolls, and with them we would make coverings to put on cupboard shelves or on mantlepieces . . . They were very beautiful things, and you didn't have to be rich to have them. I remember a great-aunt of mine, who never married. She lived in the country, in a little two-room cottage with a thatched roof and a small kitchen-garden all around it. All over the house she had those cutouts, even over the windows, instead of cotton curtains, and they were all incredibly beautiful. Her fingers were deformed from arthritis, but when she took a sheet of paper and a pair of scissors in hand, it was just spellbinding to see what she would come up with."

She looks straight into my eyes and seizes my wrist. "I am seventy-six years old," she whispers, "and I have a good memory. I know, I remember. No one can fool me, or try to make me forget that there used to be a pact between man and things. You understand me, don't you? You know what I mean. It's the same pact that's still in effect where you come from. A private, secret pact between each single individual and the things that used to be his or might one day become his. My little cutout, you beautify one corner of my life and I am grateful to you and love you for this. My little flowers on the balcony. My little felt slippers with a chain-stitch snowflake embroidered on each. My splendid leather boots that are mine only in my heart and that perhaps someday I'll be able to buy.

"Things might change—rich things, poor things, earned things, sto-len things, real things, imagined things—but the pact always remained the same. And now it no longer exists. It's over. We have the necessi-ties, that much must be said. But everything else . . . We haven't the desire to want it anymore. It's just horrible."

It is getting late. The sun is low on the horizon. Two black and white magpies are perched on the back of a bench a few steps away from us. Lyuba no longer has that artist's air that she put on at the Writers' Union. She seems like a little old lady who stepped out of a fairy tale, a little fairy godmother without any powers. I notice that her eyes are full of tears and would like to comfort her, but I don't know what to say. Ante knows her country as well as she does, and sees the same things: but for him this world—which she calls horrible—is governed by the only law capable of guaranteeing justice for man, who is malevolent by nature. And here among the dead—to whom none of this makes any difference—that light of unwonted clairvoyance recently illuminating my thoughts now shines clear on a simple truth: they are both right. Is that possible? Yes, it's possible. Here, it's possible. But what can I do to comfort Lyuba Bogomila?

"But, this is such a beautiful place," I say to her.

"Yes. The dead are at home here. What claim to ownership of a plot of land could be more valid than to be buried in it? Maybe there is no such thing as forever; but certainly they're at home here for a good while."

We hear the tram bell ring as it gets ready to leave. We drop off the tools and climb aboard for the return into town. It is almost dark outside. We travel eastward for a bit: before us lies a flat expanse that stretches as far as the eye can see. At the very end of it, resting on the last tufts of grass, looms an enormous moon, opaque ocher in color, dry and sandy: for the first time in my life, it is not a glowing circle in the sky, but a world, a compact sphere of minerals, remote and inhospitable but real, concrete. I wish I could express to Lyuba the feeling I get upon perceiving our stage's old floodlight as something possessing the same nature, the same dignity as the earth we inhabit. It's a reversal of perspective that in a way has been building up in me since my arrival in this city, but which has been completed only now, in heart-rending fashion, on this tram clanging across the boundless plain.

My comment is, to say the least, inadequate: "What a beautiful moon," I say to her.

Lyuba sighs, says nothing.

We've almost reached town and I still haven't found a way to ask about what I'm interested in. By now I'm sure of it: my crazy suspicion that the name of Milos Jarco is for some mysterious reason forbidden is well founded. It is clearly not a good idea to talk about it on the tram. I get off with Lyuba at the Yuri Gagarin stop and accompany her to the front door of her gloomy apartment building. I pluck up my courage. "Are you sure I can't come up with you for a minute? Please be so kind as to let me come in. I really need to talk to you."

She sighs and gestures for me to follow her. We take the service elevator, walk down the shadowy corridor. Lyuba slips the key in the lock and then looks at me with imploring eyes.

"Please don't look," she says.

We enter a windowless foyer—five feet by eight feet, barely larger than the area of a tomb. Against one of its long sides is a wall-bench with a narrow table, with one place set for a solitary supper on one side; across from it sits a portable typewriter. In front of the table there are two doors, both open: one gives onto a fetid bathroom, it too without windows, the other onto a bedroom with a television set in the middle of the room and a kitchenette in one corner. The walls are an old, peeling grey, the floor a green linoleum worn out at the points of most frequent passage. No bedspread, no curtains, no shade around the yellow lightbulb. Either Lyuba is frightfully negligent or else she is the victim of something beyond her control and is right when she says that the pact between man and his things is no longer in effect here. Nothing of what I see around me is an object of love; nothing is made to stir the slightest tremor of joyful satisfaction.

"I wanted to ask you for more information on Milos Jarco," I say at once, to sidestep the obligation of commenting on the surrounding squalor. We are standing very close to each other, squeezed between the table and the bathroom doorway.

"Let's sit down," she says.

We slide in behind the table, sitting down on the bench, I at the typewriter, she at the place setting.

"I really need to know something about Milos Jarco," I repeat, "and nobody will talk to me about him. I even asked Ante Radek, who seemed so willing to help me, but could get nothing out of him."

"I would gladly help you, if for no other reason than the fact that you're Italian. I am Catholic and would give anything to go back to Assisi, just once, before I die."

Lyuba is wearing a red cardigan over her cotton dress. She is rather short, and her feet barely touch the ground. She sits with her hands folded in her lap, her shoulders hunched, her round face puckered by a sad smile. I feel towards her the same natural impulse I feel toward small children or baby animals. I wish I could pamper her, give her a gift, something that would bring her joy.

"Come as my guest. I'm serious. I'll bring you with me to Città di Castello, to the home of my paternal grandparents, and from there we can go to Assisi every day if you want. I mean it; it would be a pleasure for me. They would love it too. They're peasants in the old style, like your great-aunt . . . You would like them."

"If only I could accept your invitation! Apparently you don't understand our situation, dear child. I could fast for a year and set aside a small sum—even a large sum, for that matter—but it would still be in our currency. Do you see the problem? To travel you need dollars! And they won't give us dollars, unless one has somehow earned merits— even secret merits, like your friend Ante Radek, for example."

"Merits? My impression was that he doesn't count for anything . . . In fact, to hear him speak he seems too idealistic for the orthodoxy. Overzealous, actually."

"Officially, that's true. He has no rank, in the bureaucracy. He's probably not even a registered party member. But it so happens that he can go abroad whenever he wants, whereas I definitely cannot."

The room is too small, too hot. It's stifling, and the bathroom stinks. I feel dizzy. Is it ever possible, in this wretched city, to distinguish the truth from gossip? As in the famous logical riddle, are the natives here divided into those who always tell the truth and those who always lie, or do they all lie through their teeth whenever they open their mouths? Milos Jarco jogging in his sneakers along the Promenade and at the same time making a movie in Hollywood. The four-hundred-pound Circassian woman who, from her wheelchair, watches Voytek Miczan dance naked on the riverbank. Ante Radek, with his saintly face, a spy for the police. And the police who prohibit a poor old woman from taking a trip to Assisi. And Lyuba herself—the sweet old woman sitting across from me in her dreadful apartment—a brutal mother-killer, if I'm to go by what the Writers' Union secretary told me.

That's a bit much, though. It can't be true. Suddenly it seems essential that I verify its truth or falsity. Without warning I change the subject, unconcerned that the shift might seem strange and sudden.

"When we were in the cemetery you told me you had no family buried there. Where is your family buried then? Where's your mother, for example?"

"My mother?" she looks at me as though not understanding.

"Yes, your mother. You planted flowers on the grave of a stranger today, didn't you?"

"Yes, a complete stranger . . . What else can I do? I haven't got anyone there, my Dušan isn't buried there . . ."

"And your mother isn't either?"

"Of course not. My mother died when I was a child and is buried in Hungary. She was of Hungarian origin, and she died when visiting her parents."

I guess the secretary's story must be one of the many fantasies animating the minds of these strange people. Or is it? Whatever the case, I decide to take it as a sure thing. Lyuba Bogomila, with her sweet, aging girl's face, is *not* a murderess. So is she one of the truth-telling natives? Is everything she says true? I don't think I would go that far; I'll just limit myself to listening to her with a favorable ear.

"But tell me about Milos Jarco, please."

"Why don't you go visit him? You'll get all the information you need, right from the source."

"I had thought of that, but they told me he's away, out of the country. You yourself confirmed it for me, the other day. He's in Hollywood, apparently."

"But I was mistaken, actually. I saw him just this morning, with my own eyes. He's here in town, at home."

My heart jumps. "Here in town?" I feel that if I could speak to Milos Jarco I wouldn't only find material for my feature. In fact, the thought of the article, the very instant I begin to focus on it, slips away like a tree seen from a train. Milos Jarco, who lives and writes here and makes movies in Hollywood, would actually be able, with a mere wave of the hand, to separate the true from the false and assign everything, in the East as in the West, its proper significance: the biographies of the Church Fathers, the Circassian woman, the brass nameplate that is no longer on my door, Ante Radek's fundamentalism, Mama's tolerance, the ugliness of this apartment, the beauty of the cemetery . . . "In town? And you saw him this morning?" I repeat, obtusely.

"Of course. Come, I'll show you."

She slides laboriously out from her place and invites me to follow her into the bedroom. She opens the window, which gives onto a little balcony cluttered with things for which there is no room in the house: a broom, a scrub-brush, a bucket, two hanging wash-rags, some pots, a basket with half a head of cabbage in it and a bunch of onions.

"Lean out over here." She gestures at me with her forefinger: "Look down there."

More gloomy blocks of flats, old dilapidated houses, a few nice buildings. Farther on, the tree-lined strip of the Hapsburg boulevard. "See there, beyond the Promenade? There's a building a little taller than the rest, with a parabolic antenna on the roof . . . Do you see it?"

The antenna's lattice stands out in the moonlight.

"Yes, I see it."

"There's a lighted window, on the top floor, at the corner . . . That's where Milos Jarco lives."

I continue to stare at that luminous square as though hypnotized.

Then I shake myself out of it, and at once, as though afraid that Lyuba might change her mind or suddenly forget what she has just said, I dash into the foyer to get my purse. I pull out my pen and notebook. "Could you please give me the address?"

Lyuba goes back inside, closes the window, walks slowly back to the table.

"I don't know the address. I know he lives there—someone pointed it out to me, someone who came here to my house—but I don't know the name of the street. From here I can see that the building is situated on the other side of the Promenade and perhaps, with respect to here, a little toward the river. But the address, I'm sorry, I just don't know . . ."

I race down the stairs without waiting for the service elevator. I cross the ditch and head straight for the lighted window of a still-open store. It's a baker's shop, and the baker is selling his last loaf of bread to a girl with glasses.

"Could you tell me how to get to that large building on the other side of the Promenade, the one with the parabolic antenna on the roof?"

The baker and the girl look at each other and shake their heads. "There are so many large buildings," says the girl. "Do you mean the State Radio building?"

"No, it's an apartment building, about six or seven stories high, I think."

"There must be at least fifty buildings of that size on either side of the Promenade!"

"But this one had a parabolic antenna on the roof . . ."

"A lot of them have it. Now that they're no longer forbidden, everyone's getting them."

"It's the building where Milos Jarco lives," I say, not letting up. "It's him I'm looking for."

"Well then I think it's pretty close by, more or less directly across from here," says the baker. "Just yesterday I saw him walking the dog, in the evening. I don't think he'd wandered too far from home. Try going straight toward the Promenade, then cross it and ask around."

I do as he suggests and find myself right in front of the door to the Writers' Union. It's like a game of Monopoly where I keep getting sent back to Go without collecting my two hundred dollars.

The door is closed. It is half past eight; soon Ante will be at the Esplanade. I'll try again tomorrow morning.

9

Si qua mulier hoc proposito suo utile judicans, si virili veste utatur, ad hoc virile habitum imitetur; anathema sit.
> —Sancti Leonis Magni, *Codex canonum ecclesiaticorum,* 125

If a woman, judging it useful, should don male clothing in order to imitate male behavior, let it be anathema.
> —Saint Leo the Great, *Codex of the Canons of the Church,* 125

•

HE COMES IN THROUGH the revolving door and then stops, stock-still, on the red carpet. He's dressed in his usual manner—perforated sandals included—but looks as if he has been polished. His hair, still damp, has been brushed as much as is humanly possible and sticks to his head; only at the back of his neck do a few unyielding blond curls escape capture. He has pressed his trousers; in his hand he holds a small bouquet of wildflowers with their stems wrapped in a sheet of white paper.

"Ante," I call to him, "over here."

He crosses the lobby, stops in front of my armchair with a bow. He

— 97 —

presents me the flowers: "These are for you," he says. "I picked them behind the tannery."

"Would you like a drink?"

His pale eyes cast a terrified glance around him. "No, no. Let's get out of here."

In my room I put the flowers in a glass of water and carry them over to the desk as he follows me with his gaze, standing erect in the middle of the room with hands hanging down along the seams of his pants and a gentle smile on his lips. My heart almost aches just to look at him, so clear is the light in his eyes.

I go up to him, stand on tiptoe, take his face in my hands and give him a kiss. "You're very sweet. What a beautiful, wondrous thing that a man like you should also be so sweet."

Then I'm not sure what comes over me. What I'm trying to prove, what wrong I'm trying to right, what revenge I'm trying to take, I just don't know. I've dragged him into this place that he hates. I've persuaded him to be "flexible." Isn't that enough? On the contrary, apparently. I've taken a liking to it.

I don't know. He is returning my kiss, and the twisted, four-footed crustacean our embrace has formed begins to sidle slowly toward the bed at the back of the room; but suddenly I begin to press in another direction. The crab is now proceeding in roundabout fashion; it's turning back. As it passes before the little breakfast table a white arm springs out; at the end of the arm is a hand; the hand grabs the damasked cotton tablecloth. The crab returns to the writing desk, splits into two parts. Then immediately, as cells do when reproducing, my half also begins to split in two.

I lift up my skirts, remove my panties. I really don't know what has come over me. I sit down, turn on the tape recorder, and drape the tablecloth over my knees—like a paraplegic's blanket. Do you remember? Now the division of the cell that is Valentina is complete. The northern half rests a hand on Ante's shoulder and presses down until he is kneeling on the floor. And as he disappears under the tablecloth—where perhaps the southern half is hidden, but that doesn't concern me—she says: "There's some work I have to finish."

I rewind, erase, record; I jot a few things down in my notebook, glue some labels; my excitement is heightened by the awareness of being entirely separate from what is happening at this moment under the desk. The pleasure that begins down there ends down there and does not in any way affect my control over what I am doing up here.

Is this how you used to amuse yourself? Well, now I'm amusing myself too. If it is absolutely necessary to corrupt or be corrupted, to dominate or be dominated, to roll over to the one side or to the other, I have to say that of the two, I prefer this side. Here I'm the one who decides, who gives the orders. Ante is gentle and pure, and I'm making him play a perverse, obscene game.

Except that perhaps perversion and obscenity need favorable ground in order to take root: with Ante, they slide right off like water off a swan's feathers. After a few minutes he pulls his head and arms out from under the tablecloth, hugs me around the waist, and rests his head in my lap, looking like a Guido Reni baby Jesus.

"There's just one thing I want to tell you, then I won't disturb you anymore," he whispers. "From the moment I met you I've been thinking of nothing but you." He raises his head and looks at me solemnly in the eyes. "I love you, Valentina. Now just work in peace and don't worry about me. I'll go sit by the window and look at the trees."

And he gets up, unsullied as a little proto-Christian martyr, strokes my hair lightly and goes and sits silently in an armchair.

You, Mama, will say that such a man doesn't exist. For the natural corollary of your theory, according to which nothing is ever wrong, is that nothing is ever right either. Things—and people—are merely "different" from one another, right? There is no such thing as a scoundrel, there is no such thing as a saint. It's all the same in value.

That's how it is, don't you think? I've never heard you put it quite in those words, but this would seem to me your basic premise, the cornerstone on which your morality rests.

Well, I don't see it that way. And if I ever did, I would change my mind now. Ante is good, and that's precisely the point. Is it by any chance forbidden to use that adjective? Is it not in current use, perhaps? That would be too bad, because the ones permitted don't apply to him. Except for one. Yes, that one for certain: he *is* beautiful. He does possess this supreme Western value—you yourself would recognize it at once, with the naked eye. But aside from that, no other. He is not aggressive or stylish or blessed by success or nonchalant . . . Or anything else: I can't even recall what it is that girls say about a man, what wonderful things they tell their mothers when they talk about them in our country. This hard-line angel in open sandals has taken me so far from our logic that I don't even remember what matters any more in my own country. But you will understand, I hope. You see, he's not any of that. He's just good, and beautiful, and I love him because he's good and beautiful. It makes me feel a little embarrassed to admit it. But luckily, O tolerant, open mother of mine, I can add that he believes in prison: and he believes in it precisely because he is good and beautiful, though according to a logical-moral relation that I could never explain to you. He believes in the death penalty, in the police state . . . And that's not all: if he's a spy for the party, as I think he is, it's quite likely that at the beginning he was dogging my heels to keep an eye on me, and not for love . . .

How shall we put it? For you it's inconceivable. For you the sole living heir of bygone goodness is a garrulous good-naturedness . . . Like saying: poor thing, it's not the guy's fault, is it? Let's let him be.

My angel is different. He's in favor of coming down hard, without ceremony. How shall we put it, Mama?

10

Quicumque crediderint atque accesserint ei, signabuntur ab eo tanquam pecudes; qui autem recusaverint notam ejus aut in montes fugient, aut comprehensi exquisitis cruciatibus necabuntur.

> —Lactantius, *De vita beata*, Caput XVII, "De falso propheta"

Whosoever believes in him and follows him shall be branded by him like a sheep; whosoever instead refuses his brand shall have to flee to the hills or be captured and killed amidst refined tortures.

> —Lactantius, *The Blessed Life*, Chapter XVII, "The False Prophet"

•

"THIS IS THE TANNERY," says Ante. "It's the city's main industry."

It's hard for a factory to be pretty, but this one is downright atrocious. A nauseating stench hangs stagnant in the air. From this point on, the river in which we first embraced changes color and flows on foamy and desolate.

"Was this where you picked the flowers for me?"

"Up on that slope," he gestures with his hand. "There are still a few left sticking out between the rocks."

"Let's go get them," I say.

We climb up the hill, pick a stunted little bunch, then sit ourselves down on a smooth rock. Below us we see workers in overalls lazily pushing carts outside and within a kind of thick, transparent plastic curtain.

"It must not be very pleasant to work with this smell all around you," I comment.

Ante shrugs. "Duty and pleasure are two very distant points."

The tannery is putrid and sinister, the workers drag their feet, the sky is flat and opaque. Why on earth have we come here?

"I think it should be possible to bring them a little closer," I suggest. I can see he doesn't understand. "Duty and pleasure, that is. One must be able to bring them a little closer somehow. Otherwise, what's the use of progress?"

He looks at me and smiles. For the first time since I've known him the touching candor of his eyes is ever so slightly flecked with that sort of glancing light that one sees so often back home. I'm referring to the sort of oblique radiance that lightly alters the corners of the mouth, the color of the irises. "And which of the two would you move?"

"Oh, both of them, I guess, toward some middle point. Don't you agree?"

He lies down on the rock, hands folded behind his head. The moment of irony has already passed; his face now looks sculpted from a block of white marble without cracks or veins. The sun, weakened by the clouds, pours a shadowless, milky luminosity down upon us.

"Pleasure is like a rock, my dear. It lies where it has always lain, down in the black burrow of human greed, and in all the unclean animals that are conceived and thrive in that sewer. It is born and grows down there, and out of there it crawls. Pleasure belongs to that foul abyss: you can never remove it from there. The kind of reconciliations—public and private—that are made in your part of the world consist only of ignoble compromises . . . I know how things are over there. That's the big idea, in fact: to unite duty and pleasure, by instituting bonuses for those who do their share most diligently, right? But the fact is that your bonuses are more obscene than the failures they help you to avoid. So what's the point of it? The trick works, of course: I'm well aware of that. Even that gang of shirkers in overalls down there, who are working the very minimum necessary, would double their output from one day to the next if that gave them each the right to snatch a bigger bite for himself, to humiliate his neighbor with the spectacle of his own wealth—if we legitimized and guaranteed his aspiration to be different from the rest, to have things that not everyone has and to perpetuate this right by raising special children blessed by fate. But how can we allow such a perverse distortion of our principles? Things would function better, but only according to a logic entirely contrary to the one we have chosen. For us, the only serious incentive to productivity—aside from the conscience of each individual, which I find somewhat suspect—must always be the threat that from time to time someone will be thrown into jail for a couple of years together with anyone who has any objection to this rule. It's as simple as that. We can't go making little adjustments here and there, deluding ourselves that we can keep them under control. It's criminal idiocy to hope that it would end there. If we move even an inch away from orthodoxy, all that we've built will be reduced to nothing in five years' time. In five years we would be just like you, only shabbier."

"I suppose. Still, what you say is horrible. I could never live that way. In a world where the only bonus is avoiding punishment."

He laughs lightheartedly and takes me in his arms. "But we're talking about very serious punishments: hard labor, the death penalty, mental hospital, deportation. Avoiding them can become an exquisite pleasure, don't you see?" He kisses my hair and holds me close to him. "Are you really sure you couldn't get used to life here? Think about it. Because I love you, you know."

I don't answer. He would like me to stay with him. Perhaps they would assign him a slightly larger apartment, especially if we had children. Another three feet by six, like Lyuba Bogomila's foyer. An area I've already had occasion to measure in my mind: the area of a grave.

"You say 'I love you' a little too easily, I think," I whisper to him.

"Not at all. It's the first time in my life I've said it."

The truth is that I love him too, I think. I don't tell him, though. We are sitting atop this dusty slope, watching five or six unlucky souls at a boring job they'll have to keep at until evening, when they'll go back to their shabby, depressing homes. Tomorrow they'll start over again, and so on and so forth until old age and death. We are sitting in a ghastly place, under a dirty sky, and I think I'm sorry I chose so melancholy a day to realize I'm in love with Ante Radek, poet and moralist. In a few minutes I will accompany him to the university, and then until tomorrow I will be alone again in this absurd city.

I spend the whole day idly wandering. I'm back at the hotel around mid-afternoon, putting in order the little dossier I have gathered at the department of contemporary literature of the University and at the office of Milos Jarco's publisher. It's all stuff I could have found in Italy; there was no need to come all this way.

Toward evening I return to the neighborhood where the writer is supposed to live, according to Lyuba Bogomila. Nobody can tell me anything about Milos Jarco. Only a grocer has an opinion on the matter: "He must not be home. It's a month now since he last came to get his milk." I ask where he lives, exactly. He doesn't know. "Somewhere around here," he says, gesturing vaguely with his hand. "I'm not sure exactly where. Here nearby."

I give up. I go back to the hotel, sleep badly and wake up early the next morning with the conviction that the only thing to do is to give it a try. The idea turning round in my head is, of course, absurd, but since I'm unable to get rid of it the most logical thing is to try to verify it.

An absurd idea, but only up to a point. Indeed, how could it not pop into my head? For there *are*, in fact, some strange coincidences that have taken place here, which I can hardly ignore.

All I have to do is place a series of insignificant puzzle-pieces together and see if they form a pattern, once they are all on the same plane. In short: the porter at the first hotel said Milos Jarco was in town; so did the baker. Lyuba said the same thing, and even showed me his house from afar, pointing out his lighted window. The secretary of the Writers' Union, on the other hand, showed me his photo in the newspaper as proof that the writer was in Hollywood; Voytek Miczan didn't even give me his address, saying it was pointless to look for him; and lastly, yesterday evening, the grocer said it had been a month since Milos Jarco last came in to buy milk . . .

It is clear, therefore, that either the first group or the second is mistaken—unless they are lying. So far, nothing out of the ordinary. People everywhere make mistakes and lie; there's no reason this place should be any different on that account. But where the whole affair begins to seem truly strange is when I consider the topographical positions of my informers at the various moments in which they were giving me their contradictory information.

I take the map of the city and inscribe a small circle around the neighborhood where supposedly stands the large, seven-story modern building with the parabolic antenna. Here lives Milos Jarco. Good.

Now I mark with a "yes" each of the places I happened to be when Lyuba, the porter, and the baker told me that Milos Jarco was presently at home. All just rough approximations, of course. In fact I can't quite manage to fix the meanders of this incoherent city in my memory: I get lost very easily, I never know if I'm on one side of the boulevard or the other, the street names aren't always marked. Finding the positions on the map is not easy. Let us just say I write "yes" on the points corresponding—if I'm not mistaken—to the places I happened to be on those occasions; and I write "no"—with the same qualification—on the spots where I spoke with the secretary, with Voytek Miczan, with the grocer: with all those who told me, "No, Milos Jarco is out of the country."

I move the camp stove and the apple pie I bought this morning, then spread the map out on the desk.

The result is rather peculiar. So peculiar I decide to phone my mother.

"Everything all right?" She's already at work, behind the cash register in the café. I can hear the gurgling of the espresso machine, the tinkling of cups, the voices of customers. It's as if I were there too.

"Something strange is happening," I tell her.

"I told you to watch out for the spicy muck they eat."

"No, it's not that. I'm feeling fine. How are you?"

"Great. I've started an anti-wrinkle treatment that's just marvelous. All natural ingredients: herbs and some miraculous substance produced by bees. So what strange thing is happening?"

"You know Milos Jarco? The writer I wanted to interview?"

"Yes, so?"

"Well let me explain: this city is divided into two parts. There's a kind of boulevard that cuts it down the middle. Anyway, when I'm on one side everyone tells me Milos Jarco is in town but lives on the other side; when I cross over to the other side and get to where he's supposed to be, people tell me he's been away for month and that his house is empty."

"So ring the doorbell: that way you'll see for yourself if he's home or not."

It seems so simple. "Oh Mama," I say to her, "you have no idea what things are like here. One can never get a straight, clear answer out of anyone. I still don't even know where his house is. I get the impression nobody knows his exact address, or that nobody wants to give it to me.

They all make vague gestures from afar, saying, 'It's over that way'—and that could mean just about anywhere within a half-mile radius. But that's not the point. Did you understand what I said to you? People on this side say, 'He's around, but over there. Go to the other side and ask someone to show you the exact place.' So I go to the other side and the people there tell me he's not around. It's like a nightmare, don't you see? It's very, very strange."

"Maybe he's just not there," she says.

"But don't you realize what a paradox this is? The people on this side—"

"Don't start obsessing about the people on this side and the people on that side. Obviously his neighbors are better informed and know he's not home. There's no need to create a conspiracy out of something so silly."

I send you a kiss and hang up the receiver. You really never understand me, Mama, do you. You wear gypsy skirts, sleep in a room that looks like a fortune-teller's den, live on royal jelly and birdseed, cover your face with bee-glue, make love with the *Kama Sutra* on the bedside table, practice yoga, steam-cook vegetables, go crazy for everything that's "different" and yet you don't want to make any effort to try and understand even the literal meaning of what your daughter says to you. Why do you come out with this narrow-minded common sense only whenever *I* open my mouth? Could it be that pigheaded obtuseness is a fundamental element of maternal love, an element that has remained unaltered even in the new, alternative breed of mothers?

I go back to the desk and study the map. What the marks I have made with my felt-tip pen are telling me is preposterous: Milos Jarco is present in the city only if his presence is considered from afar; this presence then turns into absence when examined from close up.

I don't think the Writers' Union opens very early in the morning. Not before ten, surely—eleven, I'd say. The secretary's calling card tells me her place of residence is on the other side of the boulevard with respect to her place of employment: if I manage to catch her at home, before she goes to work, I could question her in the very part of town where everyone says Milos Jarco is around, goes jogging, walks his dog.

I leave the hotel at nine. I arrive at the secretary's house at nine-fifteen and ring the doorbell to the second-floor door, on which I find attached a calling card identical to the one I have, with the name Roza Keleti on it.

The person who opens the door a crack to look out with one eye at me is not, however, Roza Keleti. "What do you want?" she says. "Why don't you leave us in peace?"

"Is Miss Roza Keleti at home?"

"I'm her mother. She's already left for the day. She's gone to work. Everything's in order."

"I'm sure it is." I show her the calling card Roza gave me. "I'm a friend of your daughter's. An Italian friend. She gave me her card. I was just dropping by for a visit."

"I must beg your pardon. The way things are here, you never know. At any moment they might come and take you to the police station for questioning."

"It's I who should beg your pardon. I didn't mean to frighten you. Has it really happened that they've come and taken you to the police station? . . . I'm sorry."

"No, no, not yet, at least. But you never know. Please come in, sit down."

She's a very old woman, apparently ill, and *enormous*. I recognize her from the description the secretary of the Writers' Union gave me of the mother of Lyuba Bogomila: unwell, cumbersome, to be eliminated. My God. I shudder in horror. This woman, I fear, is not long for this world. Roza, in her mind, has already committed the matricide, attributing it to Lyuba Bogomila, and sooner or later . . . And the poor woman is worried about the police! But there's no saying this will happen either. Since I've been here I haven't once been reasonably certain about anything.

"Oh . . . I'll find her at the Writers' Union."

Roza's mother is holding a cup in her hand; with her other hand she keeps mechanically stirring the tea with a little silver spoon almost invisible between her swollen fingers. Might that cup contain the poison that leaves no trace? I step backward onto the landing. There's nothing I can do, so I prefer to know nothing about it. "Never mind . . . I'm sorry to trouble you."

I flee down the stairs, my knees trembling. At the first café I find along the street leading to the hotel, I sit at a table and order a coffee and two brioches.

11

Sic homini aliquid suum debet adscribi, sine quo rationem suae conditionis amittat.
—Lactantius, *De falsa sapientia philosophorum,*
Liber III, Caput VIII

Thus it is necessary for man that something be ascribed as his own, without which he would lose awareness of his own being.
—Lactantius, *On the False Wisdom of*
Philosophers, Book III, Chapter VIII

•

"I CAN GET NO INFORMATION at all, and even you won't help me," I say to him. We're on our island, lying at the foot of the birch tree. It's Sunday: the riverbank was teeming with people, but here there's no one. I've brought along my plaid blanket, my camp stove, two dishes, and some cutlery which I borrowed from the breakfast tray at the hotel. I've just cooked some rather unorthodox spaghetti, because the pasta one can buy here is horrible.

"Soon my visa will expire and I'll have to leave."

He holds me close to him, rests his cheek against my forehead. For a few seconds he doesn't answer. When he finally does speak there's a slight quaver in his voice, as if he is trying to hold back tears.

"Please come back and stay with me. Please."

I knew he would say that. I was expecting something of the sort, preparing myself to respond to it, and yet his words hit me square in the chest like a warm wave. He's so dear, with his hollow cheeks, his eyes like a child's. I want to let myself go, let him carry me away. I take a deep breath, as if I were about to sing an aria, but the voice that comes out has nothing musical about it.

"Here on this island, forever and ever, like Crusoe and Friday. Is that what you mean? You will fish in the river while I weave garlands of flowers. It will never be night, never winter; we will never have an attack of appendicitis; our children—a dark-haired boy with blue eyes and a blond girl with dark eyes—will come to us without my having to give birth to them, carried on water lilies floating on the water. We will never grow old, never get bored. Our music will be the song of the birds, our movies will be the cloud formations in the sky. Right?"

I tear myself from his embrace and sit up with my back against the trunk of the birch. "Don't you think I want the impossible too? It's wonderful to dream, darling, but one has to realize that life runs all twenty-four hours a day. It goes on and on continuously, always, every hour of every day . . . It's not just an anthology of sublime moments."

"Why are you angry? You mustn't be angry. The fact is that we love each other. Don't you think that should count for something?"

He's right, I'm angry. The role that I find myself forced to play doesn't appeal to me. "I'm angry because you force me to be mean. It's always miserable to have to oppose a romantic dream with common sense."

"But it's not a romantic dream. I'm not asking for heaven on earth. I want to keep teaching at the university; I want to ask the authorities to assign me an apartment with a private kitchen; I want to help you find a job suitable for you—perhaps at the conservatory, where there is an opening for an Italian teacher at the moment. Isn't all this reasonable?"

"It's reasonable for you. You can conceive of living your whole life in a house you've been 'assigned,' a word that fills me with horror. I don't even know what it's supposed to mean, but it still fills me with horror. What does it mean? That the house not only is not yours, but it's not even rented, I would imagine. Don't explain it to me, I don't want to know. I'm not like you. You're happy not to have anything of your own, not to hope of ever obtaining a bonus—except that of not being thrown into a forced labor camp—not to have any material aspirations, to work always and only for improving the general conditions and never your own; you are content to bring children into the world without wanting them to have a better future than this squalid present . . . Make no mistake: I actually admire you for all these things. I revere you. I consider you a saint. But I'm not like that. If I look at myself through your eyes—if I look at my country, at everybody, in fact—it's not a pretty sight. We want to own things. We begin with wanting the things that everyone has, so we can catch up with them. Then we start wanting things that nobody has, because those are the only things of value. We want color TVs and VCRs. We want a farmhouse in Tuscany or an apartment in Clavière. We want a car for every member of the family. And while we're at it, we also want a yacht. And a personal airplane. We want romantic love, always renewed. We want sex guaranteed until age eighty. We want talent, intelligence, and money. We want designer clothes. We want success for ourselves and triumph for our children, who have to be all at least six feet tall—five feet nine for the girls—blond, and the best at tennis, at judo, at classical and modern guitar, at ballet, and at their regular studies. And just for good measure, we also want furiously to 'be,' with the accessory right to disdain 'having.' We want, in a word, an exceptional life. All of us want it, as if it were some sacred right. And we're all in the race, each in his own way. Some are more alert and get there sooner, some stop before the end. The ones who stop usually wax philosophical about it, saying they wanted to stop, but nobody ever believes them."

He takes in my tirade with the face of a child for whom Santa Claus has just been unmasked. "You can't all be the same. You're not like that . . . There must be differences."

"Of course there are. But they hold true for us, for our logic. Not for yours."

I shrug my shoulders and light a cigarette. He is now standing a few steps away, dusting the sand off his pants. It is the same scene, in grotesque reversal, I lived through ten years ago at Lambro Park, under the boughs of the nettle tree.

"It's different for you," I continue. "Where I come from, there seems to be a great deal of difference between the fact that some people, to have all these things, are willing to rob and kill and others are not. From your point of view, however, if the only real sin is cupidity, what's the difference? The modus operandi might be different but the crime is the same. It's not a pretty picture, but that's the way we are. And that's the way I am. I, mind you. I'm not talking about the society I live in, but about myself. Let me be honest with you, my angel. I, like everybody, am part of this logic. The picture I painted for you was supposed to be a portrait of my ex-husband—the kind of things one always says about others, you know what I mean. But in all sincerity, I must confess it could easily be a self-portrait too, believe me. You only have to try to imagine the same picture with the colors a bit faded—from laziness, from shyness, from a lack of outstanding gifts, an inability to oppose the greed of others, a fundamental respect for the Ten Commandments . . . There, you can say: that's Valentina Barbieri."

He kneels next to me and buries his head in my lap, wrapping his arms around my waist.

"No, no . . . If anything, yours is like an old vice that you haven't yet tried to rid yourself of . . . Don't you feel how happy we are together, even though we have nothing?"

"But don't you feel how much we wish we had something?" I reply. "Why have we come back to *this* very island, if not because we like to pretend it's ours? Why did we decide to bring the blanket here and cook our lunch if not to make as if we were in our own home? Come on, darling, let's talk seriously now: why, instead, don't you come to Italy, where one can actually have a decent life?"

He shakes his head against my lap without answering.

"I've been preaching for an hour and you won't even bother to say you disagree?"

"You know I won't leave this place. I believe in the regime we have here."

"And you have to stay to defend it, I assume."

"Yes. And now more than ever. Everyone seems crazed . . . there's an atmosphere of change that frightens me. I'm afraid there are very few of us left who know that if you give in one iota, pretty soon there will be nothing left. You can't let in the germ and not expect it to destroy, in a flash, everything we believe in. Because I do believe in it, you know."

"Yes, I know. For your information, I believe in it too. And my mother believes in it, my ex-husband believes in it, and my ex-husband's lover believes in it. If you come to Italy and talk to people in certain kinds of circles you'll find that we all believe in it. But to live in it, that's another story. I wouldn't be able to stand it. Not in so total a fashion as this. I could tolerate the poverty, the hard work, but not the principle."

White clouds drift across the sky, fraying at the edges. I continue to speak, stroking his hair. "I'm not like you. I don't identify body and soul with the morality that governs my country. On the contrary: I don't even like it. I didn't like it before I met you, and now I like it even less. I have always wanted to believe there was another way—neither this way nor that way. Another possibility . . . A kind of promise that people of good will should make to themselves. I believed . . . in the future. But now, you see . . . if there really are only two paths—yours and ours—I can only survive if I choose ours."

Ante bolts suddenly upright, propping himself up on an extended arm, and looks at me straight in the eyes. He studies me in silence for several seconds.

"What's wrong?" I ask.

Without answering he gets up on his feet and begins frantically to gather our things. "What's wrong?" I repeat.

"Let's go. I want to take you somewhere. I want to show you something." I remain seated a little longer, looking at him against the blue and white sky. Is it really man's ineluctable destiny always to lurch beyond every choice he makes? Is it possible there is no reasonable, realistic middle course, a point at which one could remain without slipping off to one side or the other and rolling progressively from bad to worse, powerless to stop? Is there nothing stable, human, or possible between ravenous greed on the one hand and the end of the pact between man and things on the other? Between making love as master and making love as servant—most often as maidservant? Between squealing and tacit complicity? Between moral frivolity and fanaticism? Between Victorian moralism and obligatory indecency?

The sole exception to this inescapable general progression toward the worst is, apparently, Milos Jarco. Like a weightless butterfly, he alighted on the razor's edge that divides the world in two, and has remained there for ten years with the utmost natural aplomb.

"If only I could interview Milos Jarco, it would be extremely important to me," I say to him. "Get that into your head. For a whole lot of reasons, believe me . . . a lot of reasons."

I'm about to lose my angel, and it's not my fault. It's not his fault either. What can we do anyway? The voice that comes out of me sounds like a little girl's: "If only I had found him, I might have understood something about this world. He would be like an interpreter, don't you think? Not like you, who are entirely on one side. I mean, he would be able to understand me too."

"But I do understand you, darling. That's why we have to go somewhere now. I'm going to take you to see something. You'll see that I understand you perfectly."

He begins to gather the plaid blanket, the camp stove, the dishes—all the furnishings of our imaginary home. I stand up and help him. We load up the boat, return to land, unload everything then load it back into the luggage rack. We work in silence. When we're back in the car, I say only: "What a shame, though, to leave so soon. We had only just arrived."

It's not enough to say "what a shame," but that's the way I talk, even to myself. Always a little below the mark. Actually, leaving the island was like dying. As he was rowing toward land, I sat with my back to him, my eyes fixed on the receding island; and I felt it was a time to utter—if only I'd been able to—some particularly meaningful, even dramatic words: the sort of things one says at moments of last good-byes. The look on Ante's face when he said "I'm going to take you to see something" makes me think that soon I'll be faced with a revelation destined to change irremediably I'm not sure what terms of our relationship, to push us beyond a certain stage where the trips to the island will no longer have any meaning. Before getting into the car I turn to look at the little thicket of birch trees and willows bordered by its pretty ring of white pebbles lapped by the river's blue water; I am certain that it is my paradise lost, the highest point of my short trajectory on this earth. I catch myself—for a second—praying God not to let me live beyond this moment. That's enough. Let's end the adventure now, before it all changes.

The road descends another few miles along the river, which is now yellow, foamy and smelly. We turn off to the left and then drive for about an hour along a straight road—parallel to the railway—which cuts across the endless plain, until we reach a little town at the edge of a forest.

We drive through the village and leave it behind us. We take a little road through the trees—beech trees, most of them. The underbrush is thick with heather and blueberry.

"Turn here."

"In the middle of the woods? Don't we risk getting stuck in the mud or caught on some root?"

"The path continues the same way to the end. It's fine, don't worry. It's just very narrow—but there won't be anyone else on it."

It's not a real, marked path, but rather a passage free of vegetation. Soon the heather and blueberry at the edges of our trail become more and more scrubby and spare, until they finally disappear altogether, giving way to brambles. Then the trees themselves become sparser; for a few hundred yards we cross a no-man's-land that is neither wood nor meadow nor heath. Clumps of blue-grey, claylike, naked earth, like huge clods upturned by some giant's plow, alternate with the brownish brush.

"Close your window," Ante tells me. "It's full of mosquitoes here."

Now mixed in with the brambles are ferns, ditch reeds, masses of grey virgin's bower draped like spider webs from stumps of dead trees. Here and there, in sunken hollows in the ground, are puddles of marshy water. The windshield is black with insects. The wipers are unable to clear them away. "I'll have to get out to wipe the glass," I say.

"Never mind, we're almost there. You can't imagine how the vile creatures sting."

I realize our journey is over when I find myself in front of an absurd construction standing slightly askew on four piles—cement, wood, and sheet metal thrown together helter-skelter. I stop the car.

"Here?"

"Here. You stay shut tight inside the car while I run ahead to open the door. When I call you, come running as fast as you can. And cover your face."

He's off like an arrow, waving his hands in front of his face. He opens an unlocked screen door, enters a small vestibule and closes the door behind him. Keeping a hand on the doorknob, ready to let me in, he gestures to me to join him.

I run at full tilt—and it's just a few yards—but still the mosquitoes manage to bite me, fly into my eyes, and get entangled in my hair. Ante receives me in his arms. "The main thing," he says, "is not to let them follow us inside." Moving about with difficulty inside that tiny cage of screens, we kill as many of them as possible and then Ante finally opens the wooden door—also unlocked—and shows me into the cabin.

Inside there is a kitchen range, a straw mattress with a few pillows and a checked blanket, two chairs, a table.

"What's this?" I ask.

Ante sighs deeply, as if about to tackle a difficult task. When he speaks, his voice is solemn. "This," he says, "is the only thing I can call mine. Mine. You see, I do understand you. I, too, know how important that adjective is: that's why I brought you here. To make you realize there's not such a wide gulf between us. This world is not another world, and I'm not that much different from you. Stay with me, Valentina. I love you, and you love me. Nothing else matters."

"You're not different from me?" I repeat. I look around. "This is the only thing you own and you don't even lock the door?"

"Who would ever come out here?"

He has a point. It's the ugliest place I have ever seen or imagined in the most desolate of fantasies. In the cabin there is nothing even worth stealing. "Damned if you're not different from me," I say. "How did you ever get the idea to build—was it you who built it?"

"A friend and I built it."

"How did you ever get the idea to build a cabin out here?" I wipe the dust off the table with my hand and lay my purse down on it. "What kind of wild idea was that?"

"I brought you here specially to tell you the story." He sits down on the bed. "Come. Don't stand there like that."

We take off our shoes. Ante leans back against the pillows and I lean against him, cradled in the circle of his arms. He begins to speak, keeping his lips close to my hair.

"This friend I mentioned was a schoolmate of mine since primary school. His name was Josip Buda and like me, he had a passion for literature. He wanted to become a novelist. We used to study together all the time, talking for hours, staying up late to read the great masters."

"And what about politics? In our country, not too long ago, young intellectuals talked about nothing but politics."

"No, the two of us talked about it very little. We both believed that good and evil are plain to see for those with eyes to see them. For us, all sophisticated formulations and ideological subtleties were just crutches used to hold up weak convictions. We didn't need them. Our convictions were strong, unshakable."

"So you haven't changed."

"No, not me." He kisses my hair and holds me close. "I could never change. And yet—and here we get to the focal point of the story I want to tell you—when we were both twenty years old and attending the university, something happened to us. We continued to talk about literature, art, morality and such, but we also began to feel a new kind of yearning—the very thing you were talking about—the need to be able to say: 'this is mine and belongs to nobody else but me.' We admitted it to each other gradually, and reluctantly. Because what we were doing, in fact, was recognizing in ourselves the very root of all evil—something we knew all about, for having analyzed it so many times. . . . We were like two physicians forced to realize that the gangrene had taken us by surprise and was following its inexorable course in our bodies. So you too, eh? we said to each other. We tormented our consciences terribly about it. As I said, our convictions were very strong, deep and naive. Like those of a good peasant, or a country priest. If they had been subtle and sophisticated, we would have done what everyone does: bent them to suit our purposes. But that wasn't possible. We would spend evenings drinking brandy and feeling guilty."

I am thinking of some of the one-year-old brats I've seen so many times at the neighborhood supermarket, perched on shopping carts, their tiny, imperious fingers pointing and threatening a tantrum as they demand every little snack-food, toy car, or Japanese robot they see.

"You really should come and live a little while in my country, to see what it really means to want to say, 'This is mine.' "

"Oh, I'm well aware it's very different. Our society, especially back then, clearly was not geared to stimulate that sort of thing; especially because we didn't yet have Western television to corrupt us with the constant spectacle of its worthless rubbish. And yet, like some infection carried on the wind, or rather like a malignant tumor generated spontaneously in the depths of our souls, the germ of greed forced us to acknowledge its presence in ourselves."

I giggle at him. "You use rather strong words, dear. Greed means snatching food from the mouths of widows and orphans, it means never being satisfied with the riches one has. . . . What's the harm in a couple of boys wishing they had—what? a motorbike? a stereo?"

He ignores me and proceeds. "We talked about it to the point of exhaustion. We decided to resort to a kind of vaccination. We would not give in, but we also knew perfectly well that we could never entirely overcome the temptation: we would therefore keep it under control. We would make a compromise. It would be a kind of homeopathic therapy. We would find something just for us, but something that we wouldn't have to take from anyone else, because nobody else could want it. It would be something precious to us alone, but we would keep it hidden as though everyone wished to take it away from us . . . It would acquire tremendous value, in our own eyes, precisely because of the secrecy in which we would surround it. I realize it's a ridiculous story, but you must understand, we were very idealistic, and only twenty years old."

I try to remember what I was like at twenty. I remember the moment Riccardo and I first met, my grandmother's death, a camel-color jacket with a half-belt, which looked very good on me, a trip along the Dalmatian coast, a very boring Christmas at my father's place, in Città di Castello . . . But what was *I* like? What was I thinking about? Nothing, apparently. At twenty I was thinking of nothing, at thirty probably not much more.

Ante keeps on talking. "And so, one day around that time, when we had gone into the woods to pick mushrooms, like an answer from heaven we discovered the canebrake and the marsh, saw the brambles and mosquitoes and understood at once that we had found the perfect spot in which to build our secret house."

"It would be nice," I say, "it would be the solution to everything, in fact, if we could have things without taking them away from anyone. It's the same principle as a chain letter, where they say that everybody wins and nobody loses."

Ante doesn't know what a chain letter is. I explain, and he ruminates a while, struck by the idea.

"Maybe what we were doing was fraud too. Maybe we weren't as naive as I like to think. In all probability we were trying to pull the wool over our own eyes, to build a whole logical construct without figuring out whether or not there was a real foundation beneath it. In any case, on holidays and during vacations we would take the train to the nearby village, where we would buy materials here and there, without calling attention to ourselves. We'd buy a few things at the cooperative, other things we'd buy second-hand from peasants. Then we would rent a mule and cart and carry everything out here. Before setting to work we would drink brandy until we were semi-anesthetized. The hard part was finding the right degree of drunkenness that would numb the sensation of the insect bites without taking away our strength and equilibrium.

And that's how we built this house, which has always been our secret and our pride and joy. Pasteur Cabin we called it, to remind us that it was supposed to serve as our vaccination."

"And what about your friend Josip? When does he come out here? Do you take turns?"

"He doesn't come here anymore. He doesn't need to anymore."

He says this with a tone of sorrow in his voice. I assume his friend is dead. "I'm sorry," I say.

"And there you are. Now you know everything about me."

I think of the doubts I have about Ante: I think of what Lyuba said, which may be true, about his working for the secret police; I think of how obstinately he has refused to speak to me about Milos Jarco; I think of the microphones in my room—if they are indeed there—and of the possibility that he might know about them and have kept them a secret from me.

"Do I know everything about you? For a saint you certainly are a good liar, I must say."

"Stay with me," he says. "I'll have you, you'll have me, and the two of us, to feed the serpent hiding in our consciences, we'll have this . . ." He can't bring himself to say "house," doesn't want to say "shack," so he says: ". . . this secret."

A surge of sadness brings a lump to my throat. If only I could say yes!

His smooth skin smells of summer; the circle of his arms, wrapped around my body, is warm and strong. Could I say yes? Would it be possible to limit the world to just him and me, alone and embracing, complicit on this bed, with the only thing outside a cloud of mosquitoes that can't come any nearer to bother us? Would the rickety walls of Pasteur Cabin be strong enough to cut love off from everything else? And how could they, anyway, if a great deal of what we call 'everything else' is also inside us—incompatible, shrill, jarring?

Ah, love. Love is all, they say. You may not say it, Mama—in fact, you resolutely deny it—but when you come right down to it, you haven't spent much time alone. Well, is it all, or isn't it? Pay close attention, since you never do understand me—there's one point I want to make perfectly clear: my doubts have nothing whatsoever to do with the possibility that Ante might work for the state police. It's hard to believe, but I realize I am able to love an informer who spies on people in order to send them to prison. I would never have believed it, but now I know; and I could perhaps even live with him. It's a monstrous thing, but I don't think that is the most important question here. I could ask him: "Are you or are you not a member of the secret police?" But it doesn't matter. He might answer, and then again he might not. Maybe he would lie. Nothing, however, could change my conviction that Ante Radek, spy or no, is a saint. See, Mama, how open-minded I am too? I could even use your very own words: "What gives me the right to judge him? What do I know of the motivations that led him to make that choice?" That's what you would say. But actually I'm not like you. It's not true that I'm unaware of his motives; on the contrary, I know them all too well and know that they're much nobler than the motives that lead others to become doctors, artists, teachers, or priests.

What frightens me is something else entirely, Mama, something that forces me to restrain the beating of my heart, to prevent it from shouting out yes, yes, I'll stay with you, forever, wherever, and however . . . It's that if the cardinal rule of my life, and that of his life, can only overlap at a single point: this heap of sheet metal hidden deep in the most uninhabitable of wastelands, besieged by mosquitoes, consumed by mildew—if this is the only point where my greedy capitalist logic and his noble fundamentalism coincide, will it ever be enough?

I knew it: our earthly paradise on the island has been annulled, made obsolete. It was only an imaginary meeting-point. Our real common denominator is this: a monstrosity, a horror that we decide to transform into a precious earthly possession by an act of will, veiling it in secrecy as in a children's game.

If only I could meet Milos Jarco! At this point I wouldn't even need to ask him anything. If a reconciliation of opposites exists in nature, I would find it embodied in him, and I might have to courage to stay. I should say to Ante: "Take me to him and perhaps I'll stay with you." But I can't.

"Tomorrow morning," I tell him, "I'm going to try for the last time to talk with Voytek Miczan. Afterward I'll tell you what I intend to do."

12

Sit quidam quotidianus usus in nobis, affectusque moriendi; ut per illam, quam diximus, segregationem a corporeis cupiditatibus anima nostra se discat extrahere, et tanquam in sublimi locata, quo terrenae adire libidines, et eam sibi glutinare non possint, suscipiat mortis imaginem, ne poenam mortis incurrat.

—Sanctii Ambrosii, *De Excessu Fratris sui Satyri,*
Liber II, 40

We should thus be on familiar, ordinary terms with death, and well disposed to it; so that, through that detachment from the bodily passions which we mentioned, our soul may learn to uproot itself and, uplifted as in a lofty place where earthly desires cannot reach it and entice it, assume the appearance of death, so as not to incur the penalty of death.

—Saint Ambrose, *On the Death of his Brother
Satyrus,* Book II, 40

•

I GO BACK to the Writers' Union, where I had sworn I would never set foot again.

Voytek Miczan, seated at his desk, receives me in a rather large, well-furnished office. From the open window one can see the rows of linden trees on the Promenade in the distance.

"You promised me I'd be taken care of," I say to him. I have decided to confront him without fear. What can he possibly do to me? I go and sit in front of him in a small rococo armchair upholstered in yellow damask. The smell of cold storage wafts over the desk and reaches my nostrils; I light a cigarette to envelop myself in a screen of protective smoke. The shiny mahogany desktop is cluttered: alone, in the middle, is a small folder with *Milos Jarco* written on it in large, black, old-fashioned lettering drawn with a calligraphic pen. Voytek Miczan pushes it toward me. I open it, skim through it. It's all things I've already found, things known all the world over. Exactly as I had expected. I look up at the president of the Writers' Union. He is resting his chin on his folded hands and looking at me over his glasses. I think I see a hint of a smile playing on his lips. I am certain his curiosity is aroused. Let's see what this woman is going to do next, he's telling himself. Then unexpectedly I realize he's rather amused in his curiosity, almost affectionate.

"Is this the famous material you were talking about?"

He nods without speaking.

"And you're not going to tell me anything yourself?"

"It's not my decision. There are a certain things . . . little things, of course—nothing out of the ordinary. But it's not up to me. I don't agree with this mania for secrecy, but what can you do. It's our style. You can imagine how much I care. I'm not going to be around much longer. I'm sick, my body is decomposing day by day. I'll be dead before the year's out."

"I'm sorry."

"Bah. Life's not such a picnic anyway. Even you, who are so young and pretty, have noticed that, I'm sure. It's not as if one loses something irreplaceable, in leaving this world. I'm leaving without any great regrets, but it is my duty to think of those left behind. So I must stick to my orders. It's not my place to tell you what you wish to know."

"Whose place is it?"

"Don't you know? Haven't you figured it out?" He tilts his head to the side and looks at me from the corner of his eyes. The look of amusement has gained ground on his pale face. Now even his eyes are smiling.

"Should I have figured it out? Do you mean . . . You're not trying to say it's Ante, are you?"

"No, no, I haven't said anything. Let it be. Let's not mention any names. Take this material here, write your article as best you can and invent the information that's missing. That's what everyone does, don't you know that? False information is as good as true."

I am still disturbed by what he left unsaid, for me to guess. Why should I have figured it out? How could I have, in the few days I've been here, if not by noticing, with my own eyes, something in someone I know personally? Which of my relations in this city does Voytek Miczan know about? He may know that I spoke at length with Lyuba Bogomila and with Roza Keleti, the secretary of the union; he may even have been informed of my visit to Roza's home and of my conversation with her mother. Therefore, strictly speaking, it's not entirely out of the question that he might be referring to one of them; but it's infinitely more likely he meant Ante.

"You mean that . . . We won't mention any names, if you don't want to. But am I to understand that you, president of the Writers' Union in this city, in a matter that directly concerns your duties, take your orders from a young poet—all right, sorry—that you take your orders from someone else?"

His smile beams even wider than before as his white hands flutter in a gesture of resignation. "In this country there are those who give orders and those who keep an eye on things to make sure the orders are carried out," he responds, "by everyone, including those who issued them."

"That's horrible!"

"It's necessary. It would be nice if everyone did what was right without being forced to, but unfortunately man is what he is."

"And so I have to go back to Italy with nothing to show for my efforts?"

"I'm sorry. Write another article. Try to think of another subject. And be optimistic about your career—I tell you that as if I were already speaking from the other world and could see things in perspective. I can't imagine there are many girls in your country as pretty and bright as you, with your command of Slavic languages. Forget Milos Jarco, take my advice, or rather, write an article based on this stuff here, as everyone else does."

He taps his hand on the folder and pushes it a few more inches in my direction. I keep my hands folded over my knees, making no move to accept his offer. It would be nice if at least Voytek Miczan, at the threshold of eternity, were willing to understand me. "You know," I say to him, "it's not really even a question of the article anymore. It's true I could write on something else. Actually, I suddenly realize I'm rather confident about my work prospects in general."

I cross my legs and make a casual gesture with the hand holding the cigarette. The smoke forms a question mark in the air. "The fact is, I think that in Milos Jarco I could find answers to certain questions—new questions, which have only come into my head in the last few days . . . But the harder I try to find the answers, the more the truth seems to elude me, and the more the name of Milos Jarco seems to turn into the mask of an enigma. It's discouraging, and a bit maddening, too, let me tell you. By this point my curiosity has gone well beyond my initial intentions, Mr. Miczan. And I assure you, if I ever managed to see behind that mask, I might even forgo writing the article."

His smile fades and Voytek Miczan's expression becomes more attentive.

"Are you serious?"

"Very serious."

"How much longer do you intend to stay?"

"A few days. My visa expires Saturday."

"Well, enjoy yourself, in the meantime."

This city certainly isn't Paris: what sort of enjoyment is he referring to? Apparently he knows all about Ante and me, about our trips to the island and perhaps even about the cabin. Or else since he's about to die, life itself is a source of enjoyment. He has just said the opposite, claimed he was departing gladly, but that doesn't mean much. Here everyone speaks in unison when they're together but they defend their right to diversity by wildly contradicting one another when taken separately; Miczan, perhaps, has merely perfected the game and is able to contradict even himself in the space of five minutes.

He stands up and walks me to the door. I now perceive his frosty aura in a different way. It frightens me a little—death frightens me, there's not much to do about that—but I no longer sense anything ridiculous or obscene in that cold odor. We shake hands with a sort of awkward solemnity, looking at each other in the eye with a glimmer of something that might have been friendship.

13

⌣ ⌐

Verum hic difficillima et latebrosissima gignitur quaestio, de qua jam grandem librum,
cum respondendi necessitas nos urgeret, absolvimus: utrum ad officium hominis justi
pertineat aliquando mentiri.

—Sancti Augustini Hipponensis Episcopi,
Enchiridion, Liber Unus, Caput XVIII

In truth, here arises a very difficult and complicated question about which we
have already written a large book, driven by the need to respond to the question
of whether at times the just man be faced with the moral obligation to lie.

—Saint Augustine, Bishop of Hippo,
Enchiridion, Sole Volume, Chapter XVIII

•

''YOU'RE DRUNK,'' I say to him.

"But not out of control," he replies solemnly. He clears his throat, sits
up in his chair. Outside the cabin the mosquitoes are buzzing by the
millions. "Is it really true you're no longer so keen on doing the article?
That you still want to find the answer, but not for that reason?"

"I certainly never mentioned that to you." He found out from Voytek
Miczan, no doubt. They must talk about me between themselves, over
my head, deciding whether or not to put microphones in my room.
. . . I should be indignant, but then, why bother?

"Never mind that you never mentioned it to me. It's true, isn't it? I may be drunk, but I wouldn't tell you what I'm about to tell you if I wasn't convinced that you . . ." He blows me a kiss from across the room. "Darling. So pretty, honest, and sweet . . ." He winks and nods slyly. "Right?"

"Right. What is it you want to tell me?"

"I'm going to tell you the truth about Milos Jarco. But you have to swear not to repeat it to anyone unless you render it unrecognizable—by changing the places and names."

"Changing the places and names?"

"Right."

"I swear."

"Good. I love you."

"I love you too. Now tell me the truth about Milos Jarco."

He leans his elbows on the table and rests his chin in the palms of his hands. "It all began when the old Minister of Education died and they appointed Kerny to the post, who still holds it. He was born in this city and was a childhood friend of Voytek Miczan; he too, as I mentioned once before, wants to make our culture less provincial, to open the boundaries of art and other such nonsense. If he had more power I'm sure he would even try to abolish censorship, and then we'd really see the floodgates open."

Continuing to speak, he gets up, totters to the straw bed and falls heavily onto it. I join him, remove his shoes, take off my clothes and lie down beside him.

"There was supposed to be this world PEN congress, which I've already mentioned to you, and Kerny got the idea—so they say—to send a delegation. His idea was rejected, but he obtained permission to send a few unofficial representatives as simple observers. But it wasn't so easy to find people willing to embark on such an adventure. Kerny was powerful, but in those days many looked on him as being too modern, too pro-West, to last very long. Participating in one of his initiatives might entail the risk of going down with him when his time came. In fact, the Writers' Union of the capital didn't even want to hear about the idea, and the same was true for all the other towns solicited, except for ours, which was the most remote town of all, practically cut off from human society, but which shared with its powerful fellow citizen a secret nostalgia for the world at large, a painful feeling of exclusion and a desire to be reunited with the rest of humanity. The passionate study of faraway things is one of our city's traditions, as are gossip and our dogged obsession with the most insignificant local occurrences: they are two sides of the same coin, the contrary results of the same isolation."

The association of ideas is hard to resist: I interrupt him with a ridiculous question:

"Is it true that Voytek Miczan married a Circassian woman who weighs four hundred pounds?"

He looks at me as though having trouble recognizing me. "What kind of woman?"

"Circassian."

"I don't know. Nobody knows his wife. But he, in any case, was the only one who accepted the invitation to bring two writers to New York. And he chose Josip—Josip Buda, my childhood friend, and me."

"Josip Buda and *you?* So you were there!"

"Exactly."

"What about Milos Jarco?"

"He turned up later. But let me tell things in the proper order."

"Would you like a coffee?"

"No, I'm fine as I am. Lying down keeps my head from spinning. Anyway, the three of us went to New York. The president, when he wasn't at the embassy drinking whiskey, was going to whores in Harlem. Josip and I diligently attended all the speeches and round tables; we wouldn't start drinking until after six, when the official members of

PEN had their social gatherings and we didn't know what to do with ourselves."

"Didn't you have fun?"

"It was awful. Everyone knew each other and ignored us as if we were invisible. We had never suffered such humiliation in all our lives. Then one day, there was a discussion entitled 'Fiction-writers and Poets,' which took place at the exact same time as the final game of the baseball championship. The American writers all stayed in their rooms glued to the TV sets, as did the press correspondents and agents."

"I wouldn't know what to choose between a discussion entitled 'Fiction-writers and Poets' and a baseball game on television. I probably would have gone out for a walk."

"We went to the discussion, of course. We had been brought to New York for the express purpose of attending the PEN proceedings, and our admission tickets had been paid for. But I can't pretend it wasn't a dreary day. There was the merest smattering of people in attendance. And the speakers who spoke all said the same things in different languages, unless perhaps the interpreter at the other end of my headset had somehow got stuck, like a broken record, on the first speaker. Then there were a few lame comments from the audience. Josip and I also got up, walked down the center aisle to the microphone, and each said his two cents' worth of clichés.

"The thing was already over, an usher had even come to tell us that time was up and we had to vacate the auditorium for the next conference—of organ donors or orchid farmers, I forget: each day ten different functions were held in the hotel's auditoriums. Anyway, at that moment, just before the day's moderator was about to declare the session closed, a young man stood up, went up to the microphone, and spoke for fifteen minutes in a very impassioned tone and a totally incomprehensible tongue. I turned the knob on my headset to all the possible settings for simultaneous translation but the interpreters were all dumbfounded. The unknown man ended his speech with a particularly resonant sentence: no one understood the words themselves, of course, but the voice had the ring of truth, or at the very least the sound of brilliant rhetoric. In fact the audience was swayed to the point of applauding, even though they hadn't understood a word. That is exactly how it happened, I swear to God. Later, other things happened—real, documented facts, which I'll tell you about in a minute. But the only way for me to get to these occurrences from the applause I just mentioned is to construct a bridge of hypothesis."

His drunkenness has passed. He pulls himself up to a sitting position and smooths out the sheet between us as if about to draw up a battle plan.

"It's just a hypothesis, but it's the only one possible." With his forefinger he draws a square on the white surface. "A press correspondent who until that moment had been up in his room watching the game, took advantage of a commercial break to come downstairs and have a look at the discussion he had been paid to attend; he witnessed part of the speech of the unknown man, heard the applause, and took to his heels again, so as not to miss a single minute of play. When he did his piece on the conference, having nothing else to write about, he wrote that a young delegate from an Eastern bloc country had created a big sensation with a speech in which he outlined in novel and convincing fashion the role of fiction and its specific nature as opposed to poetry. Other journalists who were supposed to be attending the conference then took his cue and—these are still hypotheses—filled the information out a little, inventing a few new details. Maybe one of them stuck his nose into the auditorium a minute earlier, when Josip or I was talking, and saw fit to give the unknown orator a nationality: ours. Then someone else came up with a name—only God knows where they dug it up, from what bizarre misunderstanding—the name of Milos Jarco. Then one by one, more or less, they reconstructed his famous speech, each convinced he was copying the others, each unaware he was the coauthor—as in the game of 'telephone'—of a brand-new reality."

"But where was Milos Jarco all this time?"

"Don't you understand? He didn't exist, until that moment!"

"He didn't exist? Do you mean the journalists invented him?"

"Exactly. And without even realizing it. They did it by carelessly plagiarizing from one another, corroborating one another's vague hints without bothering to check them, and then rounding them out more or less one by one. And altogether, with an antlike sort of collective intelligence, they managed—each of them unaware he was making something up, and convinced he was conforming to an historical truth—to put into the nonexistent writer's mouth all those famous theories on the specificity of fiction that we had all so long been waiting for but had been unable to formulate for ourselves.

"The reports appeared in the evening papers of the following day. Voytek read them and immediately summoned us to the embassy. 'Which of you two made the speech that they've attributed to this Milos Jarco?' he asked. We explained what had happened. He was very upset. In the end he phoned the minister of education and informed him that three journalists had already called the embassy asking for inter-views with Milos Jarco. The call woke the minister in the middle of the night, given the time difference; but he didn't hesitate a minute and said loud and clear that our country must not miss this chance to attract worldwide attention and that one of us two had to become Milos Jarco."

"I don't believe it."

"Well that's exactly how it happened. The president took us back to our hotel and left us alone with a bottle of whiskey and a bottle of vodka, saying that we had to work it out, however we wished, between the two of us, as long as we reached an irrevocable decision by seven o'clock the following morning."

"So what did you do?"

"We got extremely drunk. It was not an easy decision to make. On the one hand it was our duty to obey, and on the other hand we knew—I knew, and Josip knew—that becoming Milos Jarco meant ceasing to be an invisible worm ignored by all in that sparkling, tempting world. It's easy to find the moral strength necessary to scorn a system that doesn't even notice your existence; but if this same system, which you fight with all your might, begins to flatter you, recognizes you on the street, invites you on television, comes and asks you for interviews, then . . . For the first half-bottle we argued, because neither of us wanted to be Milos Jarco. For the second half we argued because we both wanted to be him. Then we attacked the vodka and retired each to his own bed to meditate in silence. In the end we took two little pieces of paper and each wrote his preference on one of them; these we took to the president so he could decide. It was dawn. We found him in his pyjamas. He read the notes, burned them both, and said to Josip: 'Get ready. Your first interview is at eleven.' "

I remain silent, trying to take in the meaning of this story.

"And who knows about this?" I finally ask.

"The minister of education, Voytek Miczan, me, and of course Milos Jarco. His previous identity has been obliterated—he was reported dead. He had no friends, except for me, nor relatives, except for his mother, who was told everything. Then last year she also died, so that just leaves the four of us, and you."

The idea of this makes me a little uneasy.

"I'm not going to have an 'accident' now, am I?"

"Don't worry. We went over you with a fine-toothed comb: we searched your bags, investigated your mother and your ex-husband, listened to your telephone calls. When you first got here asking questions about Milos Jarco we thought you already knew something and had come to open a can of worms. That's why we had you moved to the Esplanade, where we could check you out. And that is also why, to my great joy, I had to stick to you like your shadow all the time. And since we now know we can count on your discretion, it was decided it would be better to tell you everything. But now you have to forget it all. Voytek Miczan will give you everything you need for your article: information, photographs, testimonies, and so on."

"He's already given it to me. It's all stuff I already knew. And except for the last few years, it's all made up anyway."

"Of course. It had to be done, sooner or later. And before long it will all be true. We know by experience how these things work."

"I know what you mean. Creating the truth isn't all that difficult. What I don't understand is how you've managed to create talent. If Josip was an unpublishable novelist, how is it that Milos Jarco is such a great writer? Or was Josip perhaps already great and neither Voytek Miczan, you, nor he himself had ever realized it? Who's goofed here, you or the rest of the world?"

"It's hard to say. Josip, back then, probably already had the essential gift for it, even if it was hard to tell. He had the ability to devise the sorts of architectures of events, characters, emotions, and relationships which, when placed in a certain sequence, with the right gaps and peaks, the right balances and imbalances, the right rhythms and cadences, created something in which you could see, if you looked at it from the proper angle, a meaningful, memorable design . . . Something more limpid than reality—not a copy of reality, but unexpectedly, magically, its archetype . . . When he used to tell me about what he was writing, the novel was already there, so to speak. He had a mastery of the individual elements; he knew how to see the 'story' in the event, the 'character' in the person. That, I think, is . . . but then, is it really? Is that really 'the essential gift?' "

I interrupt him: " 'The kernel of the writer,' that's how my grand-mother would have said it, if she had ever given any thought to literature."

"Right, the kernel. Sometimes I'm absolutely certain that's it, and sometimes my thought starts going round in circles and in the end gets lost. One thing I know, however, is that as soon as Josip would get his marvelous architectures down on paper, suddenly there was nothing there anymore. There was no story, no character—nothing. Josip always encountered a void, an abyss, midway between his narrative outline and the finished work. Actually, though, to put it more simply, he was a young, naive provincial who had neither a natural gift for writing nor the cunning to live without it."

"Then he must have learned in a hurry. He must have learned in a day, in fact."

"Don't forget: a lot was expected of him. The world was favorably disposed toward him, and that was exactly what we were counting on."

He looks deep into my eyes, and again his gaze goes out of focus, as if the attempt to understand more than it is reasonable to understand has revived his drunkenness. "Have you ever wondered . . . I wonder about it, now and then. It comes to me like a flash, an unpleasant glare, a coarse, blinding light. Have you ever wondered if *that* could be the real kernel? I mean the expectation, the favorable disposition of the reader?"

"Do you think so?"

"No. But maybe yes. I don't know. Kerny was absolutely sure of it, and the facts, so to speak, have borne him out. In any case, all four of us started working on his manuscripts—Josip himself, Voytek Miczan, Kerny, and I—and I assure you that at those moments we were bent, or so we thought, on making the incidental seem excellent, nothing more. We all believed the essential was already there, though each of us identified it with something else. For Josip, I think it was that inner voice that told him: you are a writer. For Kerny it was the public's expectation. For Voytek it was those marvelous architectures I mentioned, which were there but which had trouble coming out. For me, the more I think about it, the more convinced I am that, then as now, only one thing mattered: it was useful to the party that Josip be a great writer. And therefore he *was* a great writer."

"Sounds easy."

"It wasn't too difficult, in fact. We were able to take off from Milos Jarco's phony speech from the conference, to use it as a guideline. And based on that, we created a style, to put it simply. Then we took Josip, put him in the saddle, whipped the horse in the crupper, and the aspiring novelist from the province became Milos Jarco."

I remain silent a few moments, trying to absorb the significance of this tale.

"Someone might think that *this* is the kernel."

"Oh, I know. But in fact it's just a gimmick."

"I imagine that by now Milos has already learned this gimmick, and can do it alone."

"Yes and no. Yes, he has learned the gimmick, but no, he can't do it alone. We still work together, but we've all become craftier, him included. It's less of an effort now. And we also have collaborators, who don't know that's what they are."

"What do you mean?"

"We've created a 'Committee for Narrative Planning,' which all the members of our Writers' Union are part of. They meet once a week to discuss things, make outlines, split hairs. Milos listens to recordings of the meetings, and whenever he hears something interesting he appropriates it."

"And they're not aware they're being systematically robbed?"

"Not in the least. They're convinced the 'Committee for Narrative Planning' is a useful organization, and their main fear is that sooner or later it will be dissolved. In the meantime they will continue to pocket their attendance tokens and remain quiet as mice. And if some idea they expressed during the meeting happens to reappear in a novel by Milos Jarco, they won't even recognize it."

I suddenly feel as if I'm on familiar ground. I smell an odor of the West in all this trickery. Suddenly the whole world seems to me like one of those family cartons of ice cream of assorted flavors when it begins to melt and all the colors and flavors run together and blend into a single, uniform grey.

"Doesn't it bother you to be part of a hoax?"

"Not at all." He looks at me straight in the eye, and I know he's not lying. "It's for the prestige of my country, and prestige strengthens the party."

There, now I know everything. I don't ask him if Milos Jarco is in town or in Hollywood, even though I now know he would be inclined to tell me the truth. What's the point? I wouldn't mind meeting Josip Buda, the childhood friend of my lover. But Milos Jarco doesn't mean a thing to me. He wouldn't have any answers, not for me. I look out of the window. The sun is about to set and momentarily imparts a tint of pink to the black cloud of mosquitoes besieging us.

14

Magna hominis miseria est cum illo non esse, sine quo potest esse.
—Sancti Prosperi Aquitani, *Epigrammatum,*
Liber Unus

It is man's great misery not to be together with that without which he cannot be.
—Saint Prosper of Aquitaine, *The Book of
Epigrams*

•

IT'S SATURDAY, and today my visa expires. I've already packed and loaded the car. Ante has classes until eleven o'clock, at which time I'll go pick him up and take him to Pasteur Cabin, where we'll stay, together, until it's time for me to head for the border. He will stay there until tomorrow evening, then return to town alone, by train.

I go down to the hotel lobby and pay the bill. As they had promised, the sum—extras included—is no more than I would have paid at the cheap hotel I selected upon my arrival. Of the people who brought me breakfast, made my bed, pushed the revolving door, and so on, I wonder who it was that searched through my belongings, listened to my tapes, recorded my telephone conversations with my mother. They all look like spies—or so it seems to me, now that I know what I know. But what does a spy look like? Certainly Ante, with his innocent eyes, doesn't look much like one.

I want to make one final tour, on foot, around the city, until it's time to pass by the university. Since I don't have to go anywhere, I can allow myself the luxury of a stroll along the Promenade. It is deserted and very beautiful; the birds are singing and the trees along the sidewalk are in bloom.

My intention is to walk straight up the boulevard as far as the thermal baths and then retrace my steps, thus avoiding the ugliness and greyness behind the double row of Hapsburg buildings. After going about a hundred yards, however, I am once again, and as usual, irresistibly drawn by the two disjointed half-cities to the right and left of the Hapsburg boulevard. I enter on one side, come back to the boulevard, then plunge in on the other side. I encounter again the smell of cabbage and laundry soap. From an almond green, seventeenth-century town house decorated with stuccowork a girl in a blue smock emerges at the head of band of children from four to six years old; with toots of a whistle she directs them toward the boulevard. A sign on the front door states that the building houses a nursery school. I enter the courtyard— it is very shabby but still full of mannered grace, with an ornamental staircase and a first-floor arcade entirely decorated with cherubs, garlands, and love knots. The air itself is a pastel color, and the square of sky, visible above, looks like the background to a rococo fresco with its two fluffy cirrus clouds in a corner.

As soon as I'm back in the street, the ugliness takes over again. No single building, including the one that houses the nursery school, is beautiful enough to maintain its beauty when immersed in the frayed connective tissue joining it to the rest; nevertheless, a few of the old houses here and there don't seem quite as sinister as I had first judged them to be. And as far as that goes, there are many that are not nearly as bad as Lyuba Bogomila's building, and are even nicer than my own condominium in Milan. If I decide to come back and marry Ante, we could try to get an apartment assigned to us here, in this part of the city, as close as possible to the boulevard—it doesn't matter whether it's on the left or the right side. Just as long as we don't end up in one of those dreadful housing projects in the Yuri Gagarin quarter.

I try to imagine what my life would be like. The thought of coming back here forever terrifies me; on the other hand, the idea that this stroll might be my last good-bye to this country fills me with nostalgia, not only for the islet on the river but also for the dusty streets, the tannery, the elevators with signs saying OUT OF ORDER.

What I've been repeating to myself ever since Ante first took me to Pasteur Cabin is that if he can manage to live and be satisfied with that shack as his only true, beloved possession, why couldn't I do the same? Now that he's told me the story of Milos Jarco, I know that he's had his chance to live a different life, and he turned it down: why couldn't I do the same?

If a single heart and a cabin already form a working combination, why should I be afraid to confront life with a full hand: a cabin, and the required pair of hearts?

I continue to zigzag through the streets until I find myself at the front door of the Writers' Union.

I climb the stairs, ring the doorbell. Voytek Miczan answers the door.

"There's no one here," he says, "not even Miss Keleti. We're supposed to be closed. I only came to put some papers in order. Please come in, make yourself comfortable."

He takes me into his office, which is immersed in shadow. Only a thin shaft of light beams through the closed shutters.

We sit down on either side of his desk, with that golden beam shining directly between us, falling with a strip of light on the mahogany desktop. The two of us are almost in darkness, and we speak in low voices.

"I know the whole story now."

"It's better that way. I assure you that if it had been up to me, I wouldn't have been so concerned with keeping the story of Milos Jarco a secret from you. By now, what would it matter, really, if the whole thing came out? Some might criticize us for the way we behaved at the time; others might find our brainstorm rather amusing. But nobody, for all that, would dream of questioning Milos's greatness as a writer. So why all this secrecy? The fact is that having a sense of humor is not one of the cardinal virtues of us communists."

"But wasn't it you who got scared when I started asking questions?"

"Me? No, no. It was Ante. He even phoned the minister of education to ask what he should do. He was afraid that something had leaked out, that someone had talked. I think he suspected I had. After all, there were only four of us who knew. He thought you perhaps had heard rumors and had come here to see if there was some way to create a scandal."

"Imagine that. I don't even follow the literary gossip in my own country."

"For my own part, I was assured on that account, once I had taken one look at you. I was certain you wanted exactly what you said you wanted. But Ante is a strange one. Rather naive, I would say. He doesn't acknowledge nuances. Mothers are always good, rich men are always evil, peasants are always wise, and foreigners are always suspect. Even his political convictions, which no doubt are crystal clear and unshakable, are elementary, like the convictions of a child. And that's why he never caught on with the official cadres of the party. They use him and depend on his loyalty, but they keep him at arm's length. He belongs to that category of souls that Hegel ironically defined as 'beautiful souls.' And you have to admit, irony aside, that he really is a beautiful soul."

"Yes. I was very struck by the story of what happened that night in New York, when he and Josip Buda decided which of the two of them would become Milos Jarco. I think Ante was very noble, very true to himself in the way he behaved."

Voytek Miczan remains silent a moment, immersed in shadow. Then he leans forward on his desk and his folded hands appear in the ray of light.

"Very cautious, I would say."

"Cautious?"

"Yes, cautious. Did he tell you about the phone call he made to me at four o'clock in the morning?"

Phone call? One could write a novel with all the things Ante hasn't told me. "No, I don't think so."

"He waited for Josip to fall asleep, then he phoned me . . . You know about *Ursa Major*, don't you?"

"I don't understand."

"He didn't tell you . . . Well, let's start from the beginning. I had chosen him and Josip, to go to New York with me, on the basis of a number of considerations. They were both good-looking boys, spoke English well, and their party loyalty was above suspicion. . . . But for neither one of them was my decision determined by anything they had done in the field of literature. Neither one had attained even the slightest notoriety."

"That I know, Ante told me."

"Josip had never managed to publish anything. He had submitted a manuscript of a novel to me, but it simply didn't work for me, even though it showed the boy had a certain talent. I told him to cut it, to speed up the beginning, to change the ending. To rewrite it, in short. It was very badly written."

"That too I know."

"As for Ante, on the other hand, we had already published a little book of his. Seven poems."

"*Ursa Major?*"

"Exactly."

"I didn't know that. Strange . . ."

"Anyway, he was clearly very fond of it, because when he called me at four in the morning it was to ask me if there was any way he could become Milos Jarco without having to give up *Ursa Major*. I said no, of course. He would have to burn all bridges with what he was before and be reborn as of that moment."

"And what did he say?"

"He didn't feel like taking the chance. He didn't want to exchange a very modest but real past for a perhaps luminous but only potential future. It was possible the interest aroused by that imaginary speech at PEN Club might evaporate in a day, and I didn't hide this from him. And that, in essence, was why he gave up on becoming Milos Jarco."

He gets up to open the shutters, letting in a wave of light. He goes over to a bookshelf, pulls out a small book, and places it before me on the desk. The cover is pink. The title and author's name are printed in slightly irregular letters, which look almost as if they had been drawn, very carefully, by hand. The *n* and the *t* in *Ante* are a bit too close together. Ante Radek, *Ursa Major*.

I skim through it. It's forty-eight pages long. The title of the first poem is "The Great White Stag."

I look up at Voytek Miczan. His eyes are kind and melancholy.

"So he wanted to take it with him into his new life," I say. "He wanted to become Milos Jarco without ceasing to be Ante Radek."

"Yes. Josip was more courageous, but he also had less to lose. Only his name, and what's a name anyway?"

I think of my front door, with no nameplate on it anymore. "A name is a lot when you lose it, I assure you. One doesn't realize it as long as one has it. I think Josip Buda was very courageous. I'm sorry to leave without having had a chance to meet him—to meet Milos Jarco, that is."

It's time to go pick up Ante. Voytek Miczan walks me to the door, kisses my hand.

"Good luck," he says.

What does one say to someone who's about to die? "Thank you," I say. I descend a few steps as he stands on the landing, watching me. I stop halfway down the flight of stairs and turn around to face him: now I know the right words to say, the only words that mean anything to all of us about to die, some sooner, some later. "Thank you," I say again. "I shall always remember you."

15

Nomen dictum quasi notamen, quod nobis vocabulo suo res notas efficiat. Nisi enim nomen scieris, cognitio rerum perit.

—Sancti Isisdori, *Etymologiarum*, Liber I, Caput VII

We say name almost as we say note, since with its sound it makes things known to us. Indeed, if you don't know the names, you will lose your knowledge of things.

—Saint Isidore, *Etymologies*, Book I, Chapter VII

•

HE TURNS TOWARD ME, making the straw mattress rustle. He takes me in his arms, twines his legs with mine. "Stay with me," he says.

He means forever. Let these limbs of ours, which entwine so well with one another, merge into a child, grow old together, give each other mutual support, and so on and so forth. That's what he means. He seeks my forehead with his lips and through my hair I still feel the soft breath of his words: "Stay with me." He caresses me methodically, from the back of my neck to as far as his arms can reach, to the hollow behind my knees. Then he crouches under the covers and completes the cycle—calves, ankles, heels—before coming back up on my front side, along my thighs, my mons veneris, my belly, my breasts, my throat, my face. It is as though he were committing my body to the memory of his hands, patrolling along a border.

"Why?" I ask him. Why indeed? Or rather, who? Who would be staying with you? Or what? What am I, here? Or: how? where? when? But "why?" is best of all, because it is all questions put together.

I won't tell him that Voytek Miczan told me about his phone call on the dawn of the day of Milos Jarco's birth. I won't tell him what I thought when I came here. Better not tell him what I've discovered either: that there's no escape for anyone, not even for him. He tried to convince me that one could live without having anything, aside from this children's toy, this pile of sheet metal besieged by mosquitoes. He tried and did not succeed. Each of us has stuck to his original idea. Let's leave it at that.

And we won't speak about the only thing that counts. His seven poems with their ugly cover and smudgy print are such a small possession: why open his eyes, if he prefers thinking he has nothing?

I free myself from his embrace and now it is I who gather him to my body. He lets himself be held, limp as the Christ in a pietà. As I'm holding him in my lap, my hands, too, make their rounds along his borders. "Why?" I kiss the hair on his head. There is no possible answer. Saying 'why' is like saying 'no,' and he knows that. Only if I let myself be driven by the wildest sort of amorous blindness could I ever stay with him.

But love is not blind; I know that now. It's panic that's blind, and is often mistaken for love. That same, irresistible urge that drove me to marry Riccardo, whom I loved so little, that made me become his drudge—in sex, in housework, and in theology—will never make me stay with Ante, whom I love so much. His head is on my shoulder, his hand on my breast. His eyes are shut; he doesn't answer.

I gently separate my body from his, stand up, get dressed. I heat up some water and make cappuccini for both of us. There are still seven packets left in the box. "I'll leave them for you," I say. We drink, he sitting up on one elbow, I standing erect next to the cot.

Whatever happens to me from this moment on, nothing will ever erase the image of his rib cage from my memory—the whiteness of the skin, the lightly hinted play of muscles, the tender frailty of the bones just visible through transparent flesh, the darker shadow of the stomach cavity. It was from a man's rib cage that God extracted Eve, according to Genesis; it was through Christ's rib cage that his earthly life left him, according to the gospels. That part which lies between the waist and collarbone is not entrails or brains, instinct or will. Might it be the soul, I wonder? In Ante Radek's case, it would seem to coincide: his rib cage resembles what I have come to know about him, resembles what he is. It is defenseless, noble, pure. And at the same time, it is invincibly strong.

I grab my purse and my glasses. I make as if to give him a kiss.

"You stay inside," I tell him.

But he drops his cup to the floor, gets up and frantically slips on his pants.

"Wait," he says. From a crooked shelf full of papers, boxes, and cans he immediately pulls out, without looking, a little book with a pink cover. "I want you to have this," he says. He holds it out to me, gripping it in both hands so that I can read his name and see the *n* and *t* too close together. It is a solemn offering, and I accept it solemnly. It's not merely something of his: it's his name, a bridge between past, present and future, that thing that has always remained the same though the cells of his body die and are reborn *ex novo* seven times each year—or rather once every seven years, which itself is enough to give one vertigo just thinking about it. It's the one thing he didn't want to exchange, his only true, priceless property. He follows me to the car, which is already loaded up with my luggage, air mattress, stove, blanket, water bottles, and everything else. We say good-bye hastily, under the assault of the mosquitoes. "Run back in the house," I say to him, tapping on the car window. We look at each other momentarily through the glass, as if one of us—I'm not sure which—were a human being and the other a fish enclosed in an aquarium.

I start the car up, and suddenly you're gone.

I've crossed one border now, then another, then still another. Now I'm back in Italy. Now you're the one I talk to, my darling.

I know that nothing will be the way it was before. I am returning after a winter spent in the trenches, an adventure through space. At the end of my journey there is my mother, my job, my few, distracted friends, my ex-husband, my front door with no name—as well as a piece of paper and a felt-tip pen for making a temporary nameplate while I order a new one made of brass. There are my six embroidered sheets, and my six printed cotton sheets. There is my meager bank account. There is my walnut table. There is my membership to the film club. There are people, streets, pots and pans, trolleys, stairs, and trees that belong to me in part or in whole; they are not "me" but are points outside of me that fall into place in fairly reasonable fashion so as to form, more or less, an outline that finally, when seen from the slopes of the Alps, seems easily identifiable to me. There is the certainty of having learned almost nothing, because there's hardly anything to learn aside from the fact that things might very well be destined inevitably to roll to one side or the other, since no third choice exists in nature. Not even Milos Jarco really exists, being half the accidental fruit of a misunderstanding and half a forgery created by the minister of education. And so? No matter. If that's how it is, that's how it is, and there's not an office in all the world where one might lodge a complaint. What matters is that I am not like you. I have to behave—after my own fashion—as though the proper balance were a workable hypothesis. And if it turns out not to be, what can I do about it, my love?

The familiar veil of fog rises up to meet me from the Po river plain, ready to soften mercifully any lights too bright, any thoughts too clear. The little pink book, sitting on the seat next to me like a passenger, speaks and listens to me as if it were you, my angel, now mine forever.

And to help me bear the lump that rises in my throat from knowing you are mine yet so far away, and to overcome my dismay at all the incomprehensible horror that surrounds us, I have the newfound conviction that everything is in fact so senseless that it's not worth making a tragedy out of it. For if you have the patience to push yourself far enough, you'll arrive at the comforting conclusion that at precisely the point where the last illusion falls, comedy begins.

About the Author

FRANCESCA DURANTI's novel, *The House on Moon Lake*, was a literary triumph, winning the Bagutta Prize, the Martina Franca Prize, and the City of Milan Prize. Her next novel, *Happy Ending*, was a bestseller in Italy. Ms. Duranti has a law degree from the University of Pisa and has translated novels from French, German, and English. She lives in Milan, Italy.

About the Translator

STEPHEN SARTARELLI, poet and translator, received the PEN/Renato Poggioli award for translation from Italian in 1984. A volume of his poetry, *Grievances and Other Poems* (Gnosis Press), was published in 1989.